BIG

Mike Sherer

BIG HOLE

DOUBLE DRAGON

Chapter 1 - Arrival

Snow streaked out of the black void into the high-beam headlights and back out into the black like exotic particles in an accelerator winking briefly into existence then winking back out. A subcompact rocked from the gale that propelled the flakes. The insubstantial vehicle slid slowly over snow-banked roads through a small town shrouded in darkness. Shadowy buildings with only a few scattered pinpoints of feeble illumination hunkered down against the onslaught. Not another car braved the road, and the few parked ones the little car passed appeared to be behemoth sport vehicles and pick-up trucks. The young man driving had eyes riveted ahead and both hands gripping the wheel.

A woman in her thirties seated in back stared with concern out into the demonic snow-globe of a world someone had shaken way too hard. Eileen's long lean form appeared exhausted. Her short sun-bleached hair framed a weary worried well-tanned face. It had been a long flight from Tucson, Arizona, to Missoula, Montana. Then a two-hour Uber ride from the airport up into this mountain wilderness. Then this blizzard. In May! It had been in the nineties when she boarded the plane. When she landed there hadn't even been snow on the ground. There hadn't been any in the air, either, until twenty minutes ago. Then all hell had broken loose.

From out of the whiteout loomed a shadowy structure with lights beckoning from the front windows. The car slid up before it between two parked hulking SUV's. The driver heaved a sigh of relief. "You're here."

Eileen peered out the windshield to see the front of a narrow single-story wood building with two windows and a door. The wooden sign banging about above the door and illuminated by one of the aforementioned feeble pinpoints was boldly inscribed - The Buckhorn Saloon. "Where is here?"

"Darby, Montana." The driver was enswirled with snow upon opening his door. He propelled his subcompact body out and around to the back of the car. Eileen gathered her thin jacket tight as she emerged from the back and staggered through the white wildness to join him. The driver wrestled a large suitcase from the trunk. Eileen pried out its twin. He slammed the trunk then they slogged through the snow with their back-bending loads up onto an uncovered weathered plank porch that offered no shelter from the ice slicing wind. Eileen set her suitcase down and fumbled with her wallet.

The driver waved his free hand. "No need. The contract to drive you here was very generous. As was the tip they already paid." He opened the door and lumbered inside with the bulging suitcase. Eileen put her wallet away, picked up the other suitcase, and stumbled in after him.

The door banged shut behind her. Jumping in fright, she looked to see a man seated near the door glaring at her. "Raised in a barn?" he growled.

Eileen looked around to see what kind of lion den she had been delivered into. The heat was stifling, the bright lights startling. Country music played on the jukebox. Antlers and animal heads and pelts adorned the walls. Rickety wooden tables and chairs were haphazardly arranged upon the warped wooden floor. An impressive

6

bar fronted with cheap metal stools ran across the back. Behind it reared a huge mirror set in a floor-to-ceiling cabinet and surrounded by an assortment of whiskey bottles.

A dozen or so whiskered men clad in rough denim and heavy flannel were crammed into this tight relatively safe haven. Intrigued by a stranger, a female, unescorted, out at night, in this weather, with suitcases, they all stared at her. The only sound from any of these fixated bar patrons was a hacking cough.

The driver took his leave and hurried out the door, slamming it quickly behind him so not to be reprimanded. Eileen, leaving her suitcases by the door, limped up to the bar. A woman behind the bar, appearing as worn as the furnishings, stared at her. "Coffee, please." As the woman turned toward the coffee maker a large golden cat crept out from behind the bar and curled up around Eileen's right ankle. She smiled at the feline attention then looked back to the barmaid. "How far am I from Big Hole Ranch?"

The silence that already had been as solid as the heavy wooden door was now honed to a knife-edge. No murmurs, no gasps, not a squeak from what must have been squeaky chairs. Even the cougher had seized control of his raw throat. Only the twangy wail of the jukebox. Eileen glanced from the rigid staring barmaid around the room to all the other rigid staring faces.

The door opened admitting another blast of wonderland white. A short slight frail young man, lightly clad for such intense weather, stood in the open doorway amid the hurtling snow. Everyone in the room immediately forgot about Eileen and turned toward him.

Yet no one inquired what kind of structure he had been raised in. Rather, they leaned back as far away from him as they could without actually fleeing, with hands settling on an arsenal of poorly-concealed weapons. Reactions totally inappropriate for the man's mild demeanor. He ignored them all and stared at Eileen. "Eileen?"

Eileen looked around at the others to take in their reaction. Then she looked to the young man. "Yes."

"I'm Oscar. From Big Hole Ranch." Oscar lifted both suitcases with ease. Yet he moved jerkily as if afflicted with arthritis or the beginning stages of Parkinson's.

Eileen turned toward the barmaid. "Can I have that coffee to go?" The barmaid, having retreated to the register where more than likely there was a gun within reach, stared with apprehension at Oscar as she shook her head no and waved Eileen away. Oscar jerked out into the storm with the luggage. Eileen shrugged then, after gently dislodging the snuggling cat from around her foot, gathered her light jacket tight and limped after him. She did her best to ignore the slicing stares she passed through.

One man stood and followed. He was wracked with coughs as he bundled his heavy coat up tight.

By the time Eileen made it through the blasting snow to the parked Jeep with interior lights on Oscar had already stowed her suitcases in back. He climbed in behind the wheel as she limped around to the passenger side. Before opening the car door a flash of light caught her eye. She saw a dark form close the door to the Buckhorn Saloon and disappear into the night to a chorus of ragged coughs. Eileen scrambled into the Jeep. "I hope it's not far."

8

"It's not."

Eileen buckled up. "Do you get this much? In May?"

"At this elevation in southwestern Montana we get everything in the spring. Snow, rain, hot, cold. It changes daily. Hourly, sometimes." As Oscar pulled out onto the street, Eileen looked back at the saloon. Faces were pressed to the windows watching their departure. "How was your trip?"

When Eileen turned her attention back to her driver she noticed his hands twitching on the wheel. "The flight was okay. The drive was long, but he could've driven a little further to the ranch."

"The roads are rough in the best of weather. Tonight? No way." Oscar smiled pleasantly as they left the small town and drove through a wilderness of white.

Eileen watched his spasmodic hands with concern as she opened her jacket to bask in the warmth of the tight interior. "Are you okay?"

"No," Oscar answered.

Eileen forced herself to look away out into the blizzard as they turned off the main road. Although it was covered in snow, the bump and jostle informed Eileen the road was unpaved. They wound their way through a dense forest. Eileen could barely make out the way ahead, but Oscar seemed to know where he was going. They continued in this fashion with Oscar intent on driving as his body jerked and twitched, while Eileen looked back and forth with mounting anxiety from her obviously ill driver out to the deadly darkness buffeting them from all directions.

Until Oscar jerked upright and went rigid. Then closed his eyes and slumped over the wheel.

Eileen screamed as the Jeep swerved off the road, rolled down a bank, and crashed into a tree. After the air bags deflated, Eileen screamed again. "Oscar!" He was splayed limply across the wheel. She shook him. No response. Eileen peered into his face. It was lax with eyes still closed. But he didn't seem injured. She could not see any blood.

Eileen watched the snow whipping through the pines in the headlight beams while attempting a call on her phone. No signal. She picked up the radio mike from the dash and turned it on. "Hello!"

"Hello yourself," a male voice responded.

"We've wrecked! We're off the road!"

"Is this Eileen?"

"Yes!"

"Are you injured?"

"No."

"Let me speak to Oscar."

"He's unconscious."

"Is he injured?"

"Not that I can see. He passed out at the wheel."

"Hold tight. I'll be right there."

"How will you find us? In this snow?"

"I can track your Jeep. Is the glass broken out?"

"No."

"Good. Cut the engine off. Don't risk carbon monoxide poisoning. But leave the lights on so I can see you once I get there. There are blankets in the back seat. There are emergency supplies back there, too, if you're hungry or thirsty. Be sure to wrap Oscar up. I won't be long. I can see you're already on the ranch." The radio went dead.

Eileen replaced the mike. As instructed, she cut the engine off and left the lights on. She leaned over into the back seat and located the blankets. Oscar never stirred as she wrapped up his limp body. Eileen bundled up in a blanket herself then sat staring out at the snow dashing through the halogen beams she had flipped to high.

A grizzly lumbered up out of the darkness. Eileen nearly screamed as she hopped around making certain all the doors were locked. The large bear ambled up to the passenger door and stared in at her. Eileen scooted all the way across the front into Oscar's lap. But the bear made no effort to gain entrance. Eileen's breathing slowly returned to normal as they stared at each other, neither making a move.

Until Eileen heard something behind her. She jerked around to find a large elk with an impressive rack peering in at her through the driver window. She jerked away to between the front seats, looking fretfully from one animal to the other. Like the bear, the elk made no further effort to reach her. A bald eagle swooped down onto the hood of the Jeep to stare in at her through the windshield. All three animals ignored each other. Their attention was focused on her. Having no other option, Eileen settled back to watch in wonder.

Until the radio crackled. "Eileen? I'm here." Eileen looked back to see headlight beams at the top of the bank. "I see your tracks going off the road. I'm coming down."

Eileen snatched up the radio mike. "Be careful. There's a bear, an elk, and an eagle here with me."

"Sure you didn't bang your head in the wreck?"

11

Wondering why she hadn't thought of that herself, she felt her head. "There's no blood, and I don't feel a lump."

"Those aren't nocturnal animals."

"Why don't you come down here and tell them that."

There was a moment of silence. Then, "I'll bring my rifle."

Eileen replaced the mike and turned around to look out the back. She saw the bobbing beam of a flashlight descend toward her. Eileen's nerve-wracked body relaxed. It had been a long weary day. She hadn't had a relaxing moment since she had run out of her apartment early that morning to rush to the airport. But now, relief. The menagerie broke up as the flashlight beam swept all around the Jeep. The bear and the elk strode off in different directions into the trees while the bald eagle took to the sky.

Eileen lowered the driver window. A male face appeared. "You saw them," she stated.

"Yes."

"I wasn't hallucinating."

"We'll discuss it later. Right now we need to get you to your cabin and Oscar some medical attention."

"Are you driving him to a hospital?"

"No. It's too far and the roads are too bad. Sarilyn can take care of him."

"You've got a doctor on the ranch?"

"Sort of." The man opened the driver door and uncovered Oscar so he could release his seat belt. "I'm Richard, by the way." He scooped Oscar up.

"Can you carry him up that bank in the snow? It's pretty steep."

12

Richard straightened and balanced the limp weight in his arms. "I've carried wounded men before." He trudged away.

When Eileen hopped out of the passenger side she looked uneasily into the dark trees. Were those wild animals still out there? What other ones might be lurking nearby?

"Don't worry about your bags." Eileen saw Richard was already half-way up the bank with Oscar. "I'll get them. Just come get in my truck." Eileen closed her door and scrambled up the bank.

The rest of the drive was uneventful until Oscar woke up. He came to just as a collection of dark buildings materialized out of the howling snow. "What happened, Oscar?" Richard asked.

He looked around in a daze at where he was and who he was with. "I passed out."

"I'll wake Sarilyn. She'll look you over."

"No. I'm okay."

"You are not okay," Richard insisted. "You wrecked."

Oscar looked to Eileen with concern. "Were you injured?"

"No," she responded.

Oscar impassively studied her face. "I apologize for causing you distress."

"She's fine, Oscar. You're the one having problems."

Oscar raised his right hand before Richard. It no longer twitched. "I'm okay." He lowered his hand. "Eileen has had a long stressful day. Let's get her settled in so she can get some sleep. I'm sure she needs it."

13

Richard shrugged. "If you insist." He climbed out from behind the wheel.

Oscar climbed nimbly from the back seat. "I've got the bags."

Shrugging once again, Richard went around the front of the pick-up truck to join Eileen. "There's little point arguing with Oscar." Richard led her through the mounting snow up onto the porch of a small cabin where a dim light burned. Eileen glanced back over her shoulder. Oscar was right behind them with both suitcases easily in hand. Richard unlocked the door and ushered her inside.

Snow swirled in along with Eileen as she entered a dimly-lit cramped living room. The sparse furnishings were old and worn. A hand to the back gently urged her further inside. Richard came in right behind. He closed the door after Oscar entered.

In the feeble light from the shaded lamp Eileen could for the first time take a good look at Richard. He appeared to be in his thirties - short and stocky with sharp penetrating eyes. Of note was an irregularity of his upper lip that even a flourishing moustache couldn't conceal. Unlike Eileen, he was well-prepared for the weather in heavy snow gear.

"We need to be quiet," Richard told her. "Nancy and Sarilyn are sleeping." He glanced back at Oscar. "That is if we're not waking Sarilyn up to play doctor." Oscar shook his head no.

"Where's my room?" Eileen asked.

"You're in it." Eileen watched with despair as Richard opened the sleeper sofa. He glanced up at her, shrugged. "It's a two-bedroom cabin. Men's cabin is the

14

same. Hank got our living room." Richard straightened. "Bathroom's down the hall. Throw the bolt behind me." Oscar had already exited the cabin as Richard turned to the front door.

"What's wrong with Oscar?" Eileen asked.

"Don't know. But whatever it is it's getting worse. First time he's ever passed out while driving." Richard grinned. "Just wait till you see Seth. The partner who will interview you later this morning. He's sicker than Oscar." Eileen's despair deepened. "It's nothing contagious. We hope."

"What about the other partner?"

Richard's grin dissolved. "Adam's healthy enough. At least physically."

Eileen sagged with more than the evident exhaustion. "What have I got myself into?"

Richard's twisted grin blossomed anew. "A pile of money. If your offer was anything like mine." Richard slipped out into the white whirlwind.

Eileen locked the door. She looked around the tight ratty room. Her mournful expression softened as her attention was drawn from the lumpy forbidding sofa bed up to the oil paintings that lined the walls. A beautiful waterfall cascading out of the mountains into a crystal clear pool, the air full of mist, sparkling rocks with a wolf perched at the top of them. A thermal mineral spring enshrouded in billowing steam and bordered by snow, the pale yellows and greens of bacteria-leeched rocks seen through the bubbling water, with an old falling-down wooden cabin in the background. A night sky streaked by dozens of lightning bolts, the open countryside cowering before the onslaught, one tree struck, another ablaze,

15

several more bolts attacking the ground, blasting dirt up into the air. A lush garden blooming in a rainbow of color filled with exotic statuary and imaginative topiary next to a large deep blue lake bounded by waist-high grasses in which bison grazed.

The next painting held her attention. A naked man posing nonchalantly full-frontal with a lopsided grin. He was definitely not a model. Middle-aged, bony and stringy without much muscle, thinning hair. A nondescript man lovingly portrayed. Eileen turned away from this painting with a smile.

Which diminished upon seeing the next painting. A young man with a wicked grin exposing dangerous teeth. Neon eyes that flashed with power. Long luxuriant hair. Strangler's hands open and curled as if caught in the act. A tall wiry body tense with diabolic intent clad in stylish evening clothes. She lingered at this painting studying every detail as if hypnotized. Even though by this point she was near physical collapse, Eileen could not take her eyes from the portrait. She was captivated.

Chapter 2 - The Interview

The next morning Eileen was sound asleep beneath heavy covers on the sofa bed when there was banging at the door. She opened her eyes and looked around in confusion. More knocking. "Just a minute." Eileen crawled out from the covers in tee shirt and panties, and walked with a limp much more pronounced than the night before across to the front door. Standing behind the door as she opened it a crack and looked out, she was blinded by a brilliant sunny day. She could perceive only a shadowy form on the porch. "Yes?" she said, playing for time as she shaded her eyes.

"It's time for your interview."

The voice she recognized as Oscar's. "It is?" She searched the room until she found a clock. Ten. She looked back out to the shadow. "I overslept."

"Understandable," Oscar replied unperturbed. "You got in very late."

"Can you give me a minute?"

"Certainly."

Eileen closed the door and hobbled over to stoop and rummage through one of her suitcases on the floor. "Are you okay, Oscar?"

"As okay as I'll ever be."

Eileen took out a paisley-print shirt, looked it over, tossed it down, selected a different style shirt, looked it over. "You gave me a scare last night."

"I apologize."

Eileen slipped the shirt on and buttoned it up. "Do you know what happened?"

"I passed out."

Eileen picked out a pair of jeans and looked them over. "Do you know why?"

"Yes. I'm dying."

Eileen froze at this. "I'm sorry to hear that." She sat on the bed and pulled on the jeans.

"It's nothing communicable."

Eileen stood to tug up and fasten her jeans then hobble over to open the front door. Oscar was patiently waiting. She stepped back as she tucked in her shirttail. "Come in and sit down."

Oscar walked in but didn't sit. Eileen limped to her suitcase to dig out a travel kit.

"That's a bad limp."

Eileen limped past him into the hall. "It's worse in the morning. It will loosen up."

"What happened?"

Eileen limped down the hall into the bathroom. As she passed the two bedrooms she saw both doors were open and the obviously lived-in rooms were vacant. "I was thrown from a horse. Fractured my hip."

"The doctor who worked on you wasn't very good."

"No, he wasn't." She closed the bathroom door and all further conversation came to a halt as Eileen ran water in the sink.

A few rushed minutes later Eileen, wrinkled clothes neatly arranged and unmanageable hair nearly managed, was escorted outside by Oscar. She was surprised at the warmth. The sun was shining brightly in a clear cloudless sky. There wasn't a hint of wind. The snow that had fallen the night before was already melting.

18

The lodge they approached on shoveled sidewalks and plowed road was an impressive two-story log structure. Counting windows, she reckoned it was ten units long and two wide. There was a wraparound porch. A towering stone chimney reared up at the near end. At present there was no smoke issuing from it, nor from the smaller chimney that emerged from the middle of the roof. Along the front were hitching posts for horses.

Oscar led Eileen in through the front entrance. The interior had the rustic touches she had expected, such as antler chandeliers hanging from the open-beam ceiling, wooden staircase with log railings, Native American rugs on hardwood floors, a large stone fireplace with a moose head mounted above it. There were concessions to comfort, too, such as the cushy leather couches and chairs, a large flat-screen TV, and the immense window presenting a wide open vista of snow-capped mountains.

No one was in the lobby or at the desk. Oscar escorted Eileen down the hall. They passed a spacious banquet room with a small fireplace, two conference rooms, and a game room with a pool table and several other amusements, all unoccupied.

At the far end of the hall Oscar ushered Eileen into a small, cluttered office which was not furnished to match the rest of the lodge décor. Seated behind a desk was Seth. Richard had been right. He seemed worse off than Oscar. Of indeterminate age, he was ashen, scrawny and shriveled, nearly hairless, trembling and scrunched up in obvious pain. His breathing was ragged. He looked her over with weak eyes behind thick lenses. "Please be seated." Eileen sat across the desk from Seth. "Coffee?

Juice? Milk?"

"Just water. Please." Oscar walked out. Eileen turned her attention to Seth. "I apologize for my appearance," she said.

"And I for mine," Seth replied.

"I got in late last night."

"The storm. And Oscar." Oscar returned with a glass of ice water. "Your appearance doesn't matter. Your skill and ability with animals does. You are well qualified and highly recommended. We'll double your current salary." Eileen froze upon receiving the glass from Oscar. "And there will be raises as you take on more responsibilities." Eileen gulped the water down.

Seth leaned back, coughing lightly. He tried to clear his throat, failed, then continued with a rheumy voice. "We are turning this ranch into a tourist destination. We are starting small. But the lodge was designed to be easily expandable. Also, we have plans for cabins and yurts to be added as the need dictates. Several campgrounds, both primitive and RV parks, are also laid out. We have purchased over five thousand acres so backpacking and dispersed camping will be encouraged."

After a brief bout of coughing, Seth struggled to continue. "You will be responsible for all the animals on our land, both wild and domesticated. There is already a sizeable bison herd, and a small herd of cattle. There are horses, wild and tame. You will catalogue the wild animals, learn their migration routes and habitats. There are grizzly, elk, moose, deer, black bear, fox, mountain lions, coyote, bobcats, badgers, eagles, hawks, osprey, and grouse. In Bright Creek is Grayling, Brook Trout,

20

Cutthroat, Rainbow and Brown Trout in abundance. Big Hole Ranch will become an outdoors lover's paradise, and will give access to the more remote reaches of the Bitterroot Mountains and Beaverhead National Forest. All around us is some of the most pristine natural beauty the lower forty-eight has to offer."

Eileen set the empty glass down on the desk. "Sounds like a lot of animals. A lot of responsibility."

"As we grow you will take on staff. But for now it is just you."

"Can I look the place over?"

Seth coughed violently. As he turned away to cover his cough, Eileen cast a concerned look to Oscar. He seemed unconcerned. Eileen returned her attention to Seth as he cleared his throat to resume speaking. "Of course. But we insist you stay on the ranch. The boundaries are clearly marked. Some of the owners of the private property that border us are upset with us being here, so it would not be good to wander off onto their land."

"I noticed that last night in town. I mentioned Big Hole Ranch in the Buckhorn Saloon and everyone in there clammed up."

"They fear such a big development will upset their way of life. But I assure you once we are established the locals will never know we're here." Oscar handed a map to Eileen. "So by all means, explore. But there is an urgent need for your reply. We plan to move quickly."

"The living arrangements are tight."

"A temporary hardship. More cabins for staff are being constructed."

Eileen picked the contract up and looked it over. "There's another partner?"

21

"A silent partner. You won't have to deal with him."

Oscar's head began to bob rhythmically. Eileen couldn't help but stare. "Excuse me," Oscar said. He stood and walked out with head bobbing. While Seth erupted into another fit of coughing.

Looking from Oscar to Seth, Eileen frowned. But as she studied the contract her frown transformed to an uncontrollable smile.

Chapter 3 - Exploring the Ranch

Eileen walked out of the lodge deeply conflicted. Red flags abounded. The location was remote and the owners seriously ill. Yet it was a very generous salary. And she would be doing work she loved. She looked all around. The lodge and cabins were set in a deep valley amidst towering heights lined with lodge-pole pines and ringed with snow-capped peaks in every direction. Heaven on Earth as far as she was concerned. She had always loved the outdoors, although the climate of Arizona was much different than Montana. Still, she felt no ill-effect from the altitude she had gained yesterday. Eileen had always been hardy and self-reliant. She had never allowed her bad hip to slow her down.

Eileen's limp was much improved by the time she neared the large barn. A beaming sun was making quick work of last night's snowstorm. The piles of slush melting everywhere exposed thin brown grass. She paused before the barn door to unfold the map Oscar had provided. She never had a chance to study it as Hank emerged from the barn. Eileen recognized him as the naked man from the painting. He was intent on a small electrical device in hand. It was a ragtag assemblage held together by electric tape, wires, and solder. Eileen smiled as he approached. "Hello."

He stopped with a start. Looking up from the device, he noticed Eileen looking him over. He quickly reddened. "You've seen it." Eileen nodded yes. "She promised me she wouldn't display it in public."

"Who painted it?"

23

"Nancy."

"Did she do all those?"

"Yes."

"She's very good." Hank looked away, deathly embarrassed, and resumed studying his device. "What are you doing?"

Still beet red, he kept his eyes averted. "Trying to find out why we have such bad reception here."

"My cell phone wouldn't pick up a signal last night. I thought it was the storm."

"We can't pick up any signal at any time. No satellite, no TV, no radio, no phone."

"Why is that?"

"I'll let you know when I find out." Hank walked away studying his device.

Eileen walked into the barn. The horses in their stalls were disturbed by a stranger. But they grew still as she paused to look each over. Eileen approached the largest. The golden palomino quarter horse ducked its head for her to pet. Once assured the animal was tame, Eileen entered the stall. The horse remained calm as she adeptly saddled and bridled it. Eileen led the horse out of the barn, stroking it and gently talking in its ear. The horse practically purred in response.

"You aren't planning on trying to ride that thing, are you?"

Eileen spied Hank standing by the fence. "It's a magnificent horse." The placid horse stood still while Eileen swung up into the saddle.

Hank stared in disbelief. "That thing threw Richard."

Eileen continued to stroke the horse. "Richard must not know what he's doing."

24

"It threw Denver, too."

Eileen rode off. Consulting her map and compass, she was soon out of sight of the lodge. She topped a nearly snowless hill and saw a large herd of grazing bison. Beyond them a river wound down out of the distant mountains. A big lake sparkled in the bright sun, and several small ponds were splattered across the open meadow. Wild hay swayed in the breeze.

A buzzing snagged Eileen's attention. She located a quad bouncing across an open field toward her. Once it was close enough, she recognized Richard driving it. She took note of the two rifles mounted on the back of the vehicle as it pulled up. "Didn't anyone warn you about Hell Horse?"

"If you can't handle horses stay off them."

"I can handle horses. That one's a butt biter."

"She's as gentle as a baby."

Richard stared in disbelief as Eileen dismounted. "I was ready to put it down."

"That would be a crime." Eileen looked around. "The snow sure melted fast. It was a blizzard last night."

"You should have seen the rain the day I got here. I thought the road was going to wash away. And when Sarilyn arrived? The wind blew like a tornado. And Hank came in an ice storm."

"Sounds like there's a lot of bad weather here in the spring."

"Only on days when people arrive. I've never seen lightning like on the day Nancy got here."

"I saw a painting Nancy did of it."

"She's something, isn't she? Claims this place is inspiring. Says she has never painted this well before. And she's not the only one."

"Do you paint?"

"Only the sides of barns. But there are other skills." After Richard climbed out of the quad Eileen could see he had a revolver strapped to his hip. He pointed to a distant rise. "What do you see?"

"Tall grass."

"You don't see that mule deer?"

"Where?"

Richard offered binoculars. Eileen trained them on the distant hill he indicated. She saw the deer. She lowered the binoculars. There was nothing to see without them. "You're telling me you can see that deer with your naked eyes."

"You pick out something. With the binoculars."

Eileen raised the binoculars back and scanned the hillsides. She spied a black bear in some trees. "Do you see a deer in those trees?"

Richard studied where she pointed. "No. But I see a mama bear and her cubs."

Eileen yanked the glasses back to her eyes. This time she saw the two bear cubs. Eileen lowered the binoculars and stared at Richard in surprise. "How did you do that?"

"I don't know. I could never see this good before I came here." He took a deep breath then exhaled dramatically. "Maybe it's the clean fresh air. I'm from a smoggy Midwestern suburb."

Eileen handed the binoculars back. "I'll figure out how you're tricking me."

Richard laughed. "In the meantime, since you're out for a ride I'll point out some sights you shouldn't miss." Richard pointed off into the distance. "Sky Lake has the clearest cleanest water you've ever seen. Denver is fixing up a garden there."

"I haven't met him yet."

"He shoveled your sidewalk this morning. He's the grounds keeper." As Richard pointed off in another direction, Eileen unfolded her map. "About half a mile in that direction you'll find some hot springs." Richard pointed away from the mountains.

Eileen located the hot springs on the map. "There are several hot springs marked."

Richard looked at the map and pointed to one in particular. "Yes, but that's the largest." Richard pointed off toward where the black bears had been. "At the foot of those mountains is a spectacular waterfall."

Eileen smiled her appreciation. "Thank you. This map they gave me isn't very detailed."

"If you need additional directions check with Denver. He knows where everything is. Great sense of direction."

"Another special skill?"

"Makes up for his flat face." Richard climbed back into the quad. "I almost forgot what I came up here to tell you. Seeing you on the widow maker distracted me. We've got a trespasser. He came in last night during the storm."

"How do you know?"

"My job is knowing. Be on the lookout for someone lurking. Here." Richard handed a walkie-talkie to her. "Do you have a gun?"

"No."

"Would you like a gun?"

"No."

"Can you shoot a gun?"

"I was born and raised in Arizona."

"I'll take that for a yes."

Eileen raised the radio. "If I need a gun I'll call you." Richard climbed back into his quad. "Besides, if I get in trouble I'm sure you'll be able to see me. With your fantastic eyesight."

"Think about that today when you squat behind a bush." Richard started up the quad and rolled away.

Eileen looked back to her horse. "Widow maker. No way."

Eileen mounted and rode off to the lake Richard had pointed out. Riding up over a low hill, she saw a lake that was at least five acres fed by a river swollen with snow melt rushing down out of the mountains. She folded the map and gazed upon the calm clear surface reflecting the sky like a mirror. Spying a jeep parked next to a grove of trees beside the lake, Eileen urged her horse toward it.

Until she came upon a man standing just outside the trees. He was engrossed with something taking place inside the grove. Could this be the trespasser Richard was looking for? From this distance she couldn't tell much about him except he seemed young, tall and rail-thin. Eileen raised the walkie-talkie. Then stopped when she noticed the man had seen her. He smiled and waved her down toward him.

Eileen dismounted and led her horse cautiously forward. She held the radio close. But the man made no threatening moves. Her horse shivered, snorted, pranced several nervous steps. She cooed, and petted its neck to soothe it.

Eileen led her horse up to where she could see what the man was seeing. Upon a lush lawn in the midst of a newly-planted garden of flowers and vines and bushes and trees decorated with classical statuary, a naked man and woman made love. Despite herself, Eileen stared. She would guess the young couple to be in their twenties. The man was flat on his back gazing up at the woman who straddled him. As the woman moved upon him, Eileen saw a defect low on her back serious enough to be noticed at this distance.

Finally, Eileen tore her eyes away. To find the man who had beckoned now leering at her. He made obscene gestures referencing the amorous couple. Eileen raised the walkie-talkie to call Richard.

The man disappeared. Into thin air. Eileen looked all around. He was nowhere. He hadn't ducked behind cover. He hadn't run away. He was gone in a blink. She glanced back to the couple. They had not noticed her. So Eileen withdrew and led her horse quietly away. Once distant enough not to be detected by the lovers, she climbed back up onto her horse and trotted off.

Later that afternoon Eileen rode through low hills at the foot of the mountains. The roar of a waterfall could be heard, and the mist from it could be seen rising above the hill she approached. She once again unfolded her map. Wells Falls. Eileen put the map away and topped the hill. Before her was a punchbowl waterfall tumbling fifty feet out of the mountains into a large pool.

Eileen dismounted and walked to the edge of the pool to peer in. Its clear depths seemed bottomless. Her horse came up beside her to drink. Eileen stooped to dip her hand in. She was surprised by the warmth of the water. Eileen rose and walked around the pool. At the edge of the spray she extended her hand into the falling water. It was icy. What she had expected with the water coming down out of snow-capped mountains.

Something moved in the corner of her eye. She looked to see the same man she had seen by the lake now standing on the other side of the falls staring at her with a wicked grin. This time he was close enough to recognize. It was the young man Nancy had painted. He seemed even viler in the flesh. Pasty skin, long stringy blond hair down to his shoulders, so skinny as to appear emaciated. Instead of evening wear he was clad in ripped jeans and a stained faded tee shirt emblazoned with a quote - "If you think this Universe is bad, you should see some of the others." - Philip K. Dick.

Eileen never took her eyes off him as she backed away from the waterfall. Until he disappeared. Again. Before her eyes. Just like before. Only now she was close enough to be absolutely positive there was nowhere he could have gone. He was just gone. Eileen scrambled over to where he had stood. There was no sign of him. She looked all around. Nothing. At all.

This was too much. Exploring the rest of the ranch could wait. Nancy had done a portrait of this ghost. Eileen needed to find Nancy and learn who he was. She consulted her map then rode off in the direction of the lodge.

Chapter 4 - The Disappearing Man

Eileen rode up to the lodge and dismounted. After wrapping the reins around a hitching post, she walked into the lobby. As earlier that morning there was no one present. She proceeded down the hall to the office she had been interviewed in. The door was open. She looked in to find no one there, either. Walking back down the hall she checked both conference rooms and the game room. Not a soul. Back out in the lobby, Eileen seemed stumped. Until she sniffed. Someone was cooking something that smelled delicious.

Eileen followed her nose through the dining hall into a kitchen. Where she saw a woman in her forties, short and corpulent, frowning with concentration into the large pot she stirred. With her right hand. Her left hand hanging at her side seemed so badly twisted as to be useless. "Excuse me," Eileen announced herself. The woman looked up in alarm. "Sorry to startle you."

Her expression of surprise quickly morphed into a scowl. "Wait till you've been here a while. There's plenty to startle you."

"Such as people disappearing before your eyes?" The woman stared with worry. "I'm Eileen. I arrived late last night."

"I know you did. I saw you sleeping on our couch this morning." She returned her attention to the steaming pot. "The last member of our happy family. The vet."

"I'm a little more qualified than a veterinarian. I've degrees in animal husbandry, zoology, wildlife biology..."

31

"I'm more qualified than to be cooking dinner for eight. But the pay is ridiculous."

"Isn't it?" Eileen agreed. "And this place is extraordinary. More beautiful than anywhere I ever dreamed of working." She ventured further into the kitchen. "That smells wonderful."

"It should. I've cooked in some of the best kitchens in San Francisco. Ever dine at Perbacco? Or Seven Hills?"

"Sorry. I was only in San Francisco once. For a weekend. I ate at Fisherman's Wharf. Had clam chowder in a sourdough bread bowl at Boudin Bakery."

"Typical tourist fare. Perbacco and Seven Hills specialize in Italian." The woman inhaled deeply over her pot. "No clam chowder ever smelled this good."

Eileen joined her at the stove and inhaled, also.

"Ribollita," the cook continued. "It's Tuscan. I can whip it up out of anything, any leftovers, and a little rice."

Eileen smiled across the pot into her near face. "I was looking for the woman who did the paintings in our cabin."

The woman's smile faded as she leaned away from over the pot. "That's me. I dabble."

Eileen also stepped back from the stove. "Those paintings are beautiful. Scenes and people from the ranch? You've done all those since you've been here?"

The woman nodded affirmatively. "I've never painted so well."

"The man you painted. The one with clothes on. Who is he?"

The woman smiled for the first time. "The one without clothes is Henry. A dear friend." Her smile faded. "The other is Adam. The silent partner. We hardly see him. We hardly see Seth, either, since he's been so ill. We deal mostly with Oscar."

"Adam is the one who does the disappearing trick."

The woman dismissed Eileen with a wave of her hand. "He didn't disappear while sitting for me."

"In the painting he seems so ominous. Is that what he's really like?"

"I paint what I see."

"I saw a young couple by Sky Lake."

"Denver and Sarilyn. He's the grounds keeper and she manages the lodge. He is creating this gorgeous garden there. She had the day off so she went to help him."

"It certainly was beautiful. The garden, I mean."

"Denver can make roses bloom out of solid rock. And the other member of our family you've met already."

"Richard?"

The woman smiled. "He's in charge of security. Well-qualified, I hear. Former Army Intelligence, served in Iraq and Afghanistan."

"I noticed his upper lip seems twisted."

"We're all guessing war wound." Her smile grew. "Maybe you can find out for us." She returned her attention to the large pot. "Now you must allow me to work."

Eileen turned to go, then stopped at the door. "It was a pleasure meeting you...?"

"Nancy. If you must know."

"I suppose I must. Since we'll be living together."

"I don't spend much time at the cabin." Nancy looked up from the pot. "Henry has a bed in his work shed." Nancy returned to work. "I did the portrait of him to try to

33

make him feel better about himself. He was born with subcoronal hypospadias."

"Which is?"

Nancy replied matter-of-factly. "His urethra is not in the right place. It should have been corrected when he was a baby. But it wasn't. He's very self-conscious about it."

Later that evening Eileen walked out of the bathroom in the women's cabin wrapped in a towel. Entering the living room, she froze at the sight of Adam sitting on the couch watching her. "Can you pop into this cabin, too?"

Adam laughed happily. "I didn't pop in. You left the door unlocked."

"No I didn't."

"I knocked, but you were in the shower."

"No you didn't."

"What does it matter?"

"It matters because I demand privacy."

"Not much of that here."

"Will you leave?"

"We haven't had our interview yet."

"I interviewed with Seth."

"He's so sick he doesn't know what's going on."

"I'll be happy to talk with you. Give me fifteen minutes and I'll meet you at the lodge."

"I don't spend much time at the lodge."

"I need to get dressed."

"Go right ahead." Sighing with disgust, Eileen tried to keep herself covered with the towel when she stooped before her suitcase on the floor. Adam watched with interest. "Jeans and the green paisley print blouse would be nice. Dinner is not formal."

Eileen glared over her shoulder at him. "You've been through my suitcase?"

"That's a good camera you have. Are you a professional photographer?" Eileen turned back to the suitcase to pick out jeans and a blouse (not the paisley print). "I could show you some fascinating places on the ranch to photograph."

Eileen straightened with her clothes. "Can I trust you to stay in here while I go get dressed?"

"You can trust me totally, Eileen."

Eileen walked down the hall. In the bathroom doorway she stopped to look back. "How do you do that? Disappear?"

"I'm brilliant. I'm sure Seth told you that."

"Seth didn't say anything about you."

"He should have. I'm the reason we're all here."

Eileen went into the bathroom, her indignation losing out to her curiosity, and locked the door. She hurriedly dressed. When she emerged a minute later Adam was gone.

That night Eileen limped into the spacious dining room in which a single table was set for six. Seated at it were Richard, Hank and Denver. "Good to see you're still alive," Richard greeted her.

Eileen joined them. "Why do you say that?"

"After a day of riding Hell Horse."

Denver looked with surprise from Richard to Hank. "She rode Hell Horse?"

"You people don't know what a real wild horse is. Are there assigned seats?"

The naked woman Eileen had earlier seen making love to Denver, now clothed, walked in bearing a dish.

35

"Yes. Don't get between me and Denver or between Hank and Nancy."

"That leaves me," Richard said with a smile. "Sit down before you fall down."

Eileen sat beside Richard. "There's no danger of that."

"Your limp looks worse than it did this morning."

"I'm just tired, not handicapped."

Richard nodded agreeably. "Did you find Sky Lake and Wells Falls?"

Sarilyn looked up with concern as she placed the dish. "You were at Sky Lake today?"

"Briefly. I found the waterfall more interesting. Why is the water in the pool so warm while the water falling into it is ice cold?"

"There must be a hot spring at the bottom feeding into it," Denver answered with a frown.

Sarilyn, with a matching frown, walked out to the kitchen.

"What time were you at the lake?" Denver asked.

"I didn't notice the time."

"That is some garden, isn't it?" Richard said with a smirk.

"I didn't see it," Eileen lied.

Denver sighed with relief.

"What do you think about Adam?" Eileen asked.

"I've hardly seen him," Richard answered.

"I've only been here one day and I've seen him three times. At Sky Lake, the waterfall, and in my living room, which is also my bedroom, when I got out of the shower this afternoon."

"Sounds like he's seeing a lot of you."

"I was wrapped up in a towel. I went to get dressed. When I came back he was gone."

Sarilyn re-entered with another dish, followed by Nancy bearing a dish. "Tell them about him disappearing," Nancy prompted. Four pairs of eyes turned toward Eileen.

"He disappears."

"How do you mean that?" Richard asked.

"Into thin air," Nancy replied. "Before her very eyes. Like that."

"Like a magician?"

"Could be," Eileen said. "But I don't get his trick."

"If he's good you won't."

Eileen turned away from Richard. "Hank?"

"He prefers Henry," Nancy said.

"You prefer Henry," Hank corrected her. "I answer to Hank."

"How is your project coming?"

"I've started receiving a weak signal. But it's mostly static."

"You mean we might get TV?" Sarilyn asked hopefully.

"Doubt it. Radio, maybe."

"How about cell phones?" Eileen asked.

"I'm working on it. There is a lot of interference."

"Where's it coming from?"

"All around."

Everyone fell silent as Oscar walked into the room. The entire left side of his face quivered. "Is Seth too sick to dine with us again?" Nancy asked.

"Y-Y-Yes."

Nancy walked back into the kitchen.

37

"What's wrong with your face, Oscar?" Richard asked.

Oscar looked questioningly at Richard. Then felt his face. "I s-s-seem to b-be twitching-ching."

Nancy re-entered with a tray of food. "There's enough for Seth *and* you. Since you don't seem to be feeling very well, either."

Oscar took the tray with a weak smile. He walked out with the dishes rattling.

"Are our jobs in jeopardy?" Eileen asked.

"They could be," Richard said. "Seth and Oscar seem to be getting worse."

All eyes turn toward Eileen. "How is Adam doing?"

"He seems to be a total jerk. But a healthy one." Nancy sat once again, and they all began eating.

After dinner Eileen and Richard walked from the lodge toward the women's cabin. It was a cold clear night. A multitude of stars blazed in the dark sky. Richard admired them as he walked, while Eileen limped along at his side. Until he stumbled and nearly fell. "You should watch where you're walking," she said as she steadied him. "As head of security you should know to be more careful."

"Where I grew up outside of Cleveland we didn't have night skies like this."

"We have skies like this in Arizona. Out in the desert where it's not so damn cold."

"I never saw the Milky Way with my own eyes until I got to Afghanistan."

"Were you there very long?"

"Years. In Iraq, too. But I was too busy to do much stargazing. I was usually looking down so I wouldn't plant my big foot on a mine. Or looking from side to side for IED's. Most of the time when I looked up it was to check rooftops for snipers."

"So you feel safer here? Even with what all is going on?"

Richard smiled at her. "Definitely. As long as I stay away from that damn horse of yours."

Eileen smiled in return. "A hardened combat veteran scared of a horse tame enough to eat out of your hand."

"Out of *your* hand. It would bite mine off."

They resumed their leisurely stroll. "Everyone seems to be coupled up," Eileen said.

"Except for you and me."

"Do you think we're intended to be?"

"Let fate take it's course."

"I think fate is getting a lot of help here."

Richard sighed. "I agree."

"Six employees. Three women, three men. One couple in their twenties, one couple in their forties, and us, in our thirties. This arrangement took some planning."

"This ranch is a major endeavor. I'm sure they did thorough background checks on all of us." Nearing the women's cabin, female singing could be heard coming from within. "That's Sarilyn," Richard informed as they paused to listen.

Eileen made a doubting face then listened closely. Sarilyn sang without accompaniment beautifully. "She's good enough to sing professionally."

"Then why hasn't she?" Richard asked. "Unless she couldn't sing like that before she came here."

"Like your eyesight."

"And Nancy's painting. And Denver's sense of direction. And Hank's tinkering."

"Hank's tinkering?"

"He had an appliance repair business in Baltimore. That failed. He seemed bitter about it, too. But now he works on anything and everything, happy as a lark."

"So what is there about this place that brings out the best in us?"

"Don't know. But that really is a wild animal you're riding. Have animals always taken to you like that?"

"Nothing like what happened last night, with the grizzly and elk and bald eagle. But, yeah, I've spent my entire adult life around animals, wild and tame."

"So you should be very happy here."

"I'm hoping." Richard peered longingly at Eileen. She smiled. "It's been a long day."

"At least twenty-four hours." Richard backed off.

"Did you find your trespasser?"

"Not yet. But I will. Good-night, Eileen." Richard began singing as he walked away. "Good-night, Eileen, good-night, Eileen, I'll see you in my dreams."

"You're no Sarilyn."

"Sarilyn is no Sarilyn."

Eileen opened the cabin door and walked in. Sarilyn's singing was coming through the wall of the front bedroom. Nancy was seated on the couch in the living room engrossed with a sketch pad. She looked up with a frown at Eileen's entrance. "You look tired. Do you require your bed?"

"Not yet." Eileen closed the door behind her. "Does Sarilyn always sing like this?"

"Does her singing bother you?"

"No. It's wonderful."

Nancy returned to the sketch pad. "I think so, too."

"Working on a new painting?"

"Sketching one out."

"Can I see?"

Nancy shrugged. Eileen walked over to look. She saw a pencil sketch of herself in the middle of the living room wrapped in a towel, scowling down at Adam seated on the couch staring raptly up at her. "Did I capture the moment?"

Eileen studied the sketch. Then shook her head. "Not really."

Nancy studied her sketch, also. "You mean Adam didn't enjoy the sight of you appearing before him nearly naked?"

"No, you got Adam right. It's me that's wrong."

Nancy looked from the sketch up to Eileen then back to the sketch. "It sounded like you were angry with him barging into our cabin."

"I was. But I wasn't."

Nancy abandoned the sketch to examine Eileen as she tried to ascertain her meaning.

"It's like I knew I should have been angry," Eileen went on, "but I wasn't. I was surprised at him being there. But I wasn't frightened. I didn't feel threatened. Or violated." Eileen shook her head. "It's hard to explain."

"Feelings always are. But keep trying, please. I'd like to get this sketch right."

"It's like if I had walked out of the bathroom without the towel, totally naked, it would have been alright. Like there was nothing wrong with Adam seeing me naked. A man I had never met. Except to spook me when he kept

41

disappearing. And it's not like I'm a big flirt. I don't even like to wear suggestive clothes. But with Adam it felt okay. More than okay. It felt right. Actually, I seemed to enjoy it. I don't know why." She shook her head and looked away. "Now you think I'm crazy. Or a slut."

"I certainly don't think you're a slut." Nancy focused her attention back on her sketch. "Crazy? I don't know about that, way you keep talking about Adam disappearing."

Eileen sat on the couch beside her. When Nancy glanced up, she said, "I'll help you get it right." Nancy resumed working under Eileen's intense scrutiny. While Sarilyn sang a beautiful version of 'Summertime' from Porgy and Bess.

Chapter 5 - The Trespasser

The next morning Eileen, fully recovered from the ordeal of her trip from Tucson, was showered and dressed by the time Sarilyn emerged from her bedroom. Eileen learned over coffee in the tiny kitchen that Sarilyn was from a small town twenty miles north of Birmingham, Alabama. She had been working as an assistant manager at a motel when she had been hired by Seth and Oscar to manage the lodge. They had also been interested in her because she was a certified nurse's aide and was attending school to become a registered nurse. They said since the resort was so isolated that once it grew larger they would require a nurse on staff. They had offered to pay for an online course and then send her to a nearby hospital to complete her training. Until that time she would manage the lodge. She hadn't begun her online course yet because there were difficulties establishing an Internet connection. But Seth had assured her those difficulties had nearly been worked out and she would begin her course soon.

"Right now I'm bored to death," Sarilyn said as she drained her cup of coffee. "Not only is there no Internet, but there's no phone service, no TV, not even a radio signal. It's like the stone age up here. And until they open the lodge to the public there's not a heck of a lot for me to do. So I've been helping Denver with the landscaping."

Eileen had to throttle a smile at this admission, so she changed tack. "Richard mentioned the other night that you might look at Oscar. The night he passed out driving me here from town. Do you know what's wrong with him?"

"I've never examined Oscar. He won't let me. I don't blame him. I'm not a doctor, or even a nurse."

"But you are a qualified nurse's aid?"

"Hah! That means I'm *qualified* to feed, bathe and dress patients, and clean their bed pans."

"So you have no idea what's wrong with him? Or Seth?"

"All I know is what they tell me. That it's not contagious."

"How about the other partner? Adam? Is he sick, also?"

"I've never met him."

"Really? I've only been here one day and I've met him several times."

"Unlucky you. From that painting Nancy did of him he doesn't look like someone I'd want to meet." Sarilyn rose to rinse her coffee cup.

Eileen stood also, glancing at the closed bedroom door. "What time does Nancy get up?"

Sarilyn smiled at her from the sink. "She's not in there. She spent the night with Henry." Sarilyn went off to shower while Eileen limped into the living room to close up her sleeper sofa. If Nancy was not using that bedroom maybe she could take it over. Her hip would do better sleeping in a real bed.

The limp was much improved by the time Eileen walked to the lodge. Not a soul was around. Neither Seth nor Oscar were in the office. Despite what they had said, they didn't seem to be in a hurry for her to sign the contract. Having nothing else to do, she decided to further explore the ranch.

44

Her horse was pleased to see her. Hell Horse. What was Richard thinking? The men were such wusses here. Two deathly ill, the other three terrified of a perfectly tame horse. The only real man she had met here was Adam. He wasn't sick, and he didn't seem frightened of anything. While Eileen saddled Hell Horse, which she had decided to name the horse to spite Richard, she found herself looking forward to another encounter with Adam. She hoped he'd pop in soon for a visit.

Eileen rode for an hour without encountering anyone. There were only a few clumps of snow left on the ground as it was another beautiful sunny spring day. The hillsides abounded with wildflowers - yellow bells and pink bitterroots and purple larkspurs and scarlet paintbrushes. Eileen could appreciate how Nancy drew inspiration to paint in such a place as this. The floral rainbow, the blazing blue sky, the waving tall grasses, the clear crystal lakes and placid ponds and cascading streams. It was a paradise. Eileen would have agreed to work there for half the offered salary. She just wish Seth or Oscar would show up so she could sign the damn thing.

Riding up to the top of a hill, she saw a big sign posted on a tree. APPROACHING BOUNDARY OF BIG HOLE RANCH. TURN BACK. Eileen peered beyond. There was a light fog in the trees. From which a moose emerged. Since it was part of her job to catalogue the wildlife on the ranch Eileen took out her camera and snapped several shots. Until the moose disappeared back into the fog.

"It's lost."

Eileen jerked around to find Denver standing on a rock above her. "Why do you say that?"

"It's easy to get lost here." Denver scrambled down to the ground. "Get some good shots?"

"I hope so."

"Get some good ones yesterday? Of me and Sarilyn?"

"Of course not."

"You saw us."

"I wasn't the only one. Adam was there."

"He's a creep."

"I left as soon as I realized what was going on. Almost as soon."

Denver smiled, preening.

"What are you doing up here?" Eileen asked.

"Exploring. It's my day off."

"Isn't that dangerous to do alone?"

"I've done it all my life. I can find my way anywhere." Denver peered into the fog. "This is the only place I've ever got lost."

Eileen looked to the sign. "What's over there?"

"Map shows Bitterroot National Forest. If you can find it."

"National forests are usually pretty big. Why couldn't I find it?"

Denver swept his arm off in the direction of the sign. "Be my guest." He scrambled up over the rock and out of sight.

Eileen nudged her horse toward the sign. And past it. The horse became nervous as they entered the fog. It did not want to go in there. After repeated urging from Eileen's knees and soothing petting from her hands, Hell Horse crept forward. The fog grew thicker and swirled around them. Visibility was reduced to arm's length. The horse stopped. Eileen dismounted and pulled the horse forward with the reins. The fog thinned. Eileen led her horse out of the wispy fog and on out of the trees.

"Find the national forest?"

Eileen looked up in disbelief at Denver perched atop a large rock. "I'm still on the ranch?" Eileen looked behind and saw the sign.

"That fog's disorienting."

"I could swear I went straight."

"Swear all you want. You're still on the ranch." Denver jumped down out of sight. A badly-disoriented Eileen pulled out her map to study it.

Later that afternoon Eileen rode towards a small, dilapidated shack beside a large steaming hot spring in an open pasture. She dismounted and limped toward the water.

"Are you the veterinarian?"

Eileen spun around to find a man slouched against the open doorway of the shack. He was ragged and dirty, and seemed unwell. In his free hand he held an exotic sleek handgun with the barrel aimed to the ground. He nearly dropped it upon erupting in violent coughs. "Yes," she finally replied. The two studied each other as he gasped for air. "I saw you in town the night I arrived. In the Buckhorn Saloon. That was some storm."

"Opening the gate disturbs the atmosphere." The man forced himself off the door frame and staggered toward Eileen.

"What's wrong with you?"

"Traveler sickness." He stopped several paces away. "Ubik is darkly scanned by Palmer Eldritch." Eileen collapsed at his feet. The man stooped down to her.

Hell Horse charged. The man rose to confront it, but he was so weak he wasn't nearly quick and nimble enough. Before he could raise his gun he was knocked to the ground and trampled. He attempted to rise, but the horse raised on its hind legs and stomped him again and again.

Eileen roused. Seeing what was happening, she called out to the horse. The horse dropped down to all fours, but remained nervously alert and ready to attack again. Eileen crawled over to the unmoving battered body. She ascertained he was dead. After calming her horse she pulled the radio from the saddlebag. "Richard? I think I found your trespasser."

"Are you okay?"

"Yes. But he's not. You better come see. I'm at one of the hot springs, there's a shack..."

"I can locate your radio. I'll be right there."

Eileen stared at the trampled body. Then she glanced at the unusual handgun. She picked it up. The weapon glowed, hummed, and began to vibrate. Eileen flung it down and jumped back. The gun became inert.

Eileen was kneeling beside the hot spring gazing into the water when Richard rode up on his quad. The body was where it had fallen and the gun was where she had dropped it while the horse grazed in the grass. Richard climbed off the quad with a rifle. "What happened?"

Eileen rose from the hot springs and turned toward him. "He pulled a gun on me. The horse didn't like it."

Richard examined the body. "We all warned you the horse was wild."

"I won't put him down. He was protecting me. Besides, the guy looked pretty sick to start with."

"Can't tell now with these hoof prints all over him."

"He called it traveler sickness." Richard leaned over for the gun. "Be careful." Richard paused to look at her. "Something happened when I picked it up."

Richard picked the gun up. Nothing happened. "Like what?"

Eileen held out her hand. Richard gave the gun to her. It glowed, hummed, and vibrated, like before. This time she didn't drop it. "Like that."

Richard studied the gun in her hand. "Why do you think it does that?"

Eileen shrugged as she laid it down. It once again grew inert. "I don't want to find out."

Richard turned his attention to the shack. "Did you look inside? See if he had anything else of interest?"

"No. You're security. Go do your thing."

Richard started toward the shack.

"Richard?"

He stopped to look back.

"Ubik is darkly scanned by Palmer Eldritch."

There was no reaction. Other than the incredulous look Richard gave her. "Hey, I like Dick as much as the next guy, but are you sure that horse didn't get you in the head, too?" Eileen shrugged and turned back toward the hot springs. Richard studied her a moment longer then continued into the shack.

Chapter 6 - The Movie

Late that afternoon Eileen returned to the lodge on Hell Horse. She saw Richard's quad parked in front. Eileen dismounted and walked inside. Sarilyn was seated in the lobby in tears. "Sarilyn? What's wrong?"

"Seth died."

Eileen saw Nancy standing quietly in a corner. "Have the police been notified?"

"Oscar says he'll take care of it," Nancy answered.

"Oscar's not too well himself."

"Has anyone seen Denver?" Sarilyn stopped crying long enough to ask.

"I saw him this morning," Eileen said. "He's rock climbing in the mountains."

"That's his story." All three women turned to see that Hank had walked into the lobby. "He's really trying to find a way off the ranch."

"What are you talking about?" Nancy asked.

"We're prisoners here."

"I got lost in the fog this morning," Eileen said.

"You'll always get lost in the fog," Hank said. "Every time."

"You mean we can't just drive away?" Sarilyn asked, "On the road?"

Everyone grew silent as Richard entered supporting a shaky Oscar. "Oscar says Seth left a video for us. To be watched upon his death."

"Are you serious?" Eileen demanded. "Watch a movie? What about the police?"

"We can't reach the police." Richard glanced toward Oscar. "Conference Room One?" Oscar nodded erratically. Richard looked around. "Shall we?" Everyone started toward the hall.

"What about Denver?" Sarilyn asked.

"I radioed him. He's on his way in." Richard handed Oscar off to Hank then turned toward Eileen. "Are you okay?"

"Define okay. I just watched a man be trampled to death by a horse and just learned I'm being held prisoner."

"You sound okay. Let's go see what Seth has to say."

As they all filed into the conference room Hank took a DVD from Oscar. Who then collapsed into a seat. Hank inserted the DVD into the player while everyone else sat before a large flat-screen.

Denver rushed in. "Did I miss anything?"

"Seth is dead," Richard told him. "We've got a movie to watch." Dumbfounded, Denver looked around. Sarilyn caught his eye, and he sat beside her.

Hank began the video. Adam appeared on the screen with an ill-humored smile. He was standing before Wells Falls. "I know you were expecting Seth. But he's dead. I'm not. So what I have to say is more important." Everybody in the room glanced to Oscar. He sat rigid showing no reaction at all. "As I'm sure you have all figured out by now this ranch is *not* going to be a tourist destination. The only tourists who will ever come here are already here. Except for the occasional trespasser. More about them later. Now, let's talk about me." Adam strode about the pool, energized. "I am a physics graduate student at MIT. Or was, until kidnapped by Seth and

Oscar. They brought me here. Then, one by one, you arrived. And now Seth is dead, or you wouldn't be watching this. And Oscar is not far behind. So there are to be only the seven of us."

Adam started toward the waterfall. Disappeared. "That's the disappearing I was talking about," Eileen said.

"Special effects," Hank said.

"Very special."

The garden by Sky Lake appeared on screen. A moment later so did Adam. "We are prisoners. As I'm sure you realize by now. But what a prison. The larders are well-stocked, we can live for years on what has been stored away for us. Also, there is a herd of cattle, bison, game animals. Also, fruit orchards, every kind of seed to grow produce this climate will support. Many wells, springs, abundant clean water." Adam stepped toward the lake and disappeared.

"I wish he'd quit doing that," Sarilyn complained.

"He's showing off," Denver said.

Conference Room One appeared onscreen. Everyone twisted about looking for Adam. He appeared on screen, laughing. "Gotcha. I'm not here now. I filmed this earlier."

"Bastard!" Sarilyn yelled.

Adam strode through the empty room looking around at them as if they were present, which they presently were, and addressed the empty seats as if they were occupied, which they presently were. "But most importantly, you are here. What good would this elaborate set-up be if there weren't people qualified to manage it. We have Richard, adept at tracking and hunting and shooting, to take advantage of the plentiful game. Denver

52

to raise the produce. Eileen to manage the livestock. Nancy, who not only is a master chef but can also butcher and preserve food. Hank, a handy-dandy fix-it man to keep the place running. And Sarilyn, who not only can tend to our health but can also provide entertainment. But what can be the purpose of such an elaborate arrangement?"

Adam walked into the flat screen at the front of the room and disappeared. The hot springs with the falling-down shack appeared. Adam emerged from the steam of the hot spring. "Me. Why? I haven't a clue. They didn't tell me. But it's obvious they were to be the wardens, you were to be the guards, and I was to be the sole prisoner. But now the wardens are dead. Leaving the guards and the prisoner to work out a new relationship. Oh, yes, we can't forget who you refer to as the trespasser."

Adam strode toward the shack. "People can get in here. With weapons. To what purpose? To kill. Me? You? All of us? Who knows? But you can bet the man trampled by Eileen's horse won't be the last. We must defend ourselves. I propose we work together. Not only to that purpose, but to find a way out of here. If people can get in then people can get out. But how can I trust you? I don't know what lies Seth and Oscar told you about me. And there are six of you and only one of me. So we need a liaison. Eileen. I will deal only with her. I'll feel much safer dealing one to one with her."

Adam walked into the shack. The mountains appeared with a boundary sign displayed on a tree and the wall of fog in the trees beyond. Adam emerged from the fog. "In the meantime, explore. Enjoy. Settle in for a long stay. I'll be getting in touch with Eileen." Adam walked back into the fog. The screen went blank.

Richard rose and walked to Oscar. He sat unmoving with glazed eyes staring while seeming not to breathe. "Is he dead?" Hank asked.

Richard looked him over. "He appears to be."

Sarilyn came over to examine him. "He's passed out before. I wouldn't pronounce him dead yet."

Richard nodded in concurrence as he rose and looked at Eileen. "Why you?"

"I have no idea."

Sarilyn, nearly hysterical, looked up from Oscar. "Aren't we even going to try to leave?!"

"We have tried, honey," Denver said. "We can't."

"So we just give up and *live* here?!" She motioned toward the blank screen. "With *him*?!"

"No," Denver said. "I'm working on it. If there is a way out of here I'll find it."

"What about her?" Nancy motioned toward Eileen. "I definitely don't trust Adam. Am I supposed to trust her?"

"I want out of here as bad as you do," Eileen answered.

"This could be exactly the reason Adam stated he'd work only with Eileen. To sow distrust and discord. She was the last to arrive and the least known to us." All eyes turn toward Richard. "If we are at each other's throats then we won't be at his. We are dealing with a very clever man. A physicist from MIT.

"He claims," Hank said.

"So let's deal with what we *know* to be true. We have two bodies to bury. Oscar we'll keep an eye on for now. Denver, will you help me?"

54

"Sure."

"I can help, too," Hank offered.

"I want you to examine the trespasser's gun. See what makes it tick."

"What about her?" Nancy once again motioned at Eileen.

"Eileen stays with me. If Adam tries to contact her I want to be there. Sarilyn?" Richard turned to the extremely upset woman. "Are you okay?"

"She'll be okay." Nancy stood to put a consoling arm around her shoulders.

"If you are, I want you to search the lodge for Seth's movie. The one he intended us to see. If it's hidden here you'll be the one to find it. You know this lodge better than any of us."

"I'll help her look," Nancy offered.

"No. I'd like you to keep an eye on Oscar. In case he comes to."

"So I get the death watch."

"Are you up to it?"

"Certainly."

"Then let's get busy. Denver? What about your garden at Sky Lake? Good place to start a cemetery?" Denver nodded as he stood. Sarilyn slipped out from under Nancy's arm to hug and kiss him. Nancy walked over to do the same with Hank. Richard smiled at Eileen. "Do I get one?"

"Not from me." Eileen stomped out.

Chapter 7 - Hopping

Eileen sat in the Jeep Richard parked at the edge of the garden at Sky Lake. The wrapped bodies of Seth and the trespasser were strapped to the back behind her. Richard and Denver pulled out shovels and picks. "What do you think, Denver?" Richard asked.

"Over here." Denver walked into the garden.

Richard glanced back at Eileen. "Will you stay with the bodies?"

"Do I have a choice?"

"None of us have a choice. We're trapped here." He followed Denver.

Eileen spied Adam fifty yards away at approximately the same place she had seen him before. He motioned her closer. Eileen glanced over her shoulder. Richard and Denver were out of sight. She approached Adam with caution.

"It's reassuring to know people are as stupid as ever," he said. "They thought to build a prison for me. Instead they built me a fortress. This ranch is nearly impregnable. I'm safe here."

"Safe from what?"

Adam motioned toward the Jeep. "He was a hit man. Sent to assassinate me."

"If they meant to kill you why didn't Seth or Oscar do it?"

"They have become more desperate." Adam laughed. "They see their plan falling apart."

"He said something strange to me before he died."

Adam stopped laughing and grew deathly serious. "I'd love to hear it."

"Ubik darkly scans Palmer Eldritch."

"Philip K. Dick," Adam responded after brief consideration. "Other than that, I haven't a clue." He looked beyond Eileen toward the garden. "I need to inform you of an important detail I failed to mention in my movie. We can't kill each other."

"I bet my horse could."

"That was impressive. Something else they didn't think through when designing this place."

"My horse?"

"Do you recall your interview with Seth?"

"Yes."

"What did you have to drink?"

"Water."

"There was something in the water. I drank it when I first got here. The others have all drank it. We've all been poisoned."

"I don't feel poisoned."

"It's very sophisticated nanotech. It will only be activated if one of you were to kill me. As will the poison in me if I were to kill any of you."

"Insurance against us murdering each other?"

"Exactly. Now I must go. I'll be talking with you some more." Adam disappeared.

Eileen walked to the spot where Adam had been standing. There was no trace of him ever having been there. Turning back toward the garden, she saw Richard staring at her. "Did you see that?" she asked.

"Yes I did. He disappeared. Just like you said. No special effects involved." Richard walked toward her. "I also heard. We've all been poisoned so we won't kill each other. What if we die by illness or accident?" Richard stopped in front of Eileen. "Why does he talk to you?"

"Perhaps he's lonely for female companionship."

"There are two others."

"Taken."

"As supposedly you were to be. By me."

"Seth and Oscar planned this well."

"But Adam says their plans are falling apart."

"My, your ears are as amazing as your eyes."

"He's right. They're dead. And they knew they were dying. So they arranged for us to come here. To take over guarding their prisoner once they died."

"What did he do? To deserve such imprisonment."

"And why couldn't they just execute him? If he is so dangerous?"

"HEY!!" Richard and Eileen looked toward the garden. A weary and dirty Denver leaned on a shovel. "SOME HELP HERE?!!"

Richard started toward the garden. "Come supervise."

Eileen fell into step with him. "I can dig."

"You've got a bad leg."

"It's a bad hip. My right hip. I can dig with my left leg."

"Did you get back on that horse? The one that threw you when you were a kid?"

"Of course." Eileen and Richard joined Denver at the partially-dug grave.

Once the two corpses were interred, the three drove back to the lodge. Denver went into the lodge to shower, while Eileen and Richard walked to Hank's work shed. It was littered with electrical components, wiring, and scattered tools of all shapes and sizes.

Hank looked up from studying the weapon as they entered. "It doesn't work."

"It works," Richard replied. "For Eileen." Both men turned toward her.

Eileen picked up the gun. It glowed, hummed, and vibrated, as before. She laid it down and it died.

"Have you fired it?" Hank asked.

"No," Eileen replied.

"How are we going to find out what it can do if you don't fire it?" Hank asked.

"And it seems that you are the only one who can," Richard said. "It does nothing for me." He turned to Hank. "Why is that?"

"Maybe it's a security protocol," Hank answered. "Since she was the first to touch it after its previous owner died it will now only work for her."

"What would be secure about that?" Richard asked Hank. He turned to Eileen. "Did you notice how well the grip fit your hand?"

"Not really. I was too worried it was going to blow up in my hand." Both men glared at Eileen. Until she picked it up again. It reacted to her touch as before. She tested the feel of the weapon in her hand.

"Why would the trespasser be carrying a gun that fits Eileen's hand so well?" Richard asked.

"Maybe he wasn't," Hank said. "Maybe it conforms to its user."

"Pretty sophisticated. More sophisticated than any gun I've ever encountered."

"You've encountered that many guns?" Eileen asked.

"Yes. I've been in personal security since I got out of the Army."

"A bodyguard."

"Call me that and I'll call you a veterinarian."

The door burst open and Nancy rushed in, distraught. Seeing the glowing gun in Eileen's hand, she grew more distraught and screamed. "What is that?!"

Eileen laid the gun down, and it died.

"What's wrong?" Hank asked Nancy.

Nancy stared at the inert gun a moment longer then looked to Hank. "Oscar's gone."

"You were supposed to watch him," Richard growled.

"I watched him for an hour. He never budged. So I went to help Sarilyn look for the other movie. When I checked back on him he was gone."

"So he woke up and walked off," Hank said. "He can't go far."

"Can't go far?" Richard snarled. "This ranch is over five thousand acres."

"We'll find him." Hank reached for Nancy, and she collapsed in his arms.

Richard sighed. "I guess that means Sarilyn hasn't found the movie yet."

"I'll help her look," Eileen said.

"While we search for Oscar. Hank?"

Hank ignored Richard.

Nancy wiped away a tear. "Go on. I'll start dinner."

"You're still cooking?" Hank asked.

"We have to eat. No matter what. Besides, it will keep me calm." Nancy broke away and walked out.

Hank glared at Richard. "I'd be careful how I speak to the woman who cooks my food."

"Why? I've already been poisoned." Seeing that Hank was intrigued, he continued, "I'll tell you about it while we look for Oscar." Richard glanced back at Eileen. "Coming?"

Eileen started toward the door. "Shouldn't I give Denver a chance to finish his shower before I start prowling through the lodge?"

"Why? You've seen him naked before."

"She has?" Hank said. "Man, I miss all the good stuff."

Eileen laughed. "Seeing Denver naked sounds good to you?"

"That's not what I meant!" Hank sputtered as the three walked out of the shed.

Eileen began her search of the lodge upstairs. Behind one closed door she heard the shower running, and could also hear Sarilyn's voice as she conversed with Denver. So she walked down the hall to explore the next room.

Eileen encountered Adam in the third room she entered. She had just finished searching the closet when she turned and saw him seated on the bed watching her. She nearly screamed. "Don't do that!" she said, collapsing into a chair.

"Did you ever consider that the solution to a problem is the problem?"

"What's the solution to you hopping around like you do?"

"Tinkering with the boundary."

"What?"

"I thought you were asking how I do it?"

"I wasn't. But I will."

"The boundary to the ranch warps space. You walk into the boundary, continue in a straight line, then walk out at the same place you walked in. How is that possible? If you did indeed continue in a straight line? The space you walked through was curved. Like traveling around the world. Continue in a straight line, and you'll eventually arrive back where you started."

"If you've figured out the boundary why haven't you escaped?"

"I've learned to manipulate the boundary a little, but I can't pass through it."

"How do you manipulate it?"

"Use the curved space to create wormholes. Like secret passageways in an old Gothic house between rooms which don't appear to be connected."

"So you can pass through these secret passageways to anywhere on the ranch."

"No, only through the passageways I've established. I'll construct more in time. Seems like I'll have plenty of time."

"Is there a passageway to this room?"

"No. It's in another part of the lodge."

"So what's to stop me from grabbing you and holding you until the others come?"

"To what purpose? Other than it sounds like it might be fun."

"What purpose? How about me beating some answers out of you."

Adam spread his arms wide. "No need for violence. What do you want to know?"

"What did you do?"

"Nothing."

"Then why did Seth and Oscar go to such lengths to imprison you here?"

"My turn."

"What?"

"I answered your question. Now answer mine." Eileen nodded agreement reluctantly. "How old were you when you injured your hip?"

"Five. Now answer mine."

"Seth believed I'm going to do something terrible. Do you remember the accident?"

"Of course. What are you going to do?"

"I haven't the foggiest. What kind of horse was it?"

Eileen grew still. "I don't remember. I was five."

"Ask me something. So I can ask you if you remember limping before the accident."

"What are you getting at?"

"Maybe falling off a horse wasn't the cause of your injury. Maybe you were just told that. At five you'll believe anything." Eileen jumped up from the chair and paced across the room. "Is this upsetting you?"

"Being trapped here? Of course it's upsetting me."

"This is a beautiful place. You're surrounded by the love of your life, animals. You have interesting companions. Including me."

"A comfortable cage is still a cage."

"Of course it is. So help me break out. You and me. Forget the others."

Eileen stopped pacing to confront Adam. But he was gone. She lunged across the room out into the hall. It was empty. She sagged against the door frame.

That evening the six gathered in the dining room for the meal Nancy had prepared. They all quietly stared into the centers of their plates as they ate. Richard looked up with a weak smile. "This is very good, Nancy."

"Of course it is," she muttered.

Richard looked around. Not having sparked any conversation, he resumed eating.

Following the doleful dinner, Richard and Eileen walked from the lodge toward the women's cabin. Her limp was so pronounced Richard stepped up to support her, but she wouldn't allow it. Overhead was another glorious starry night with the myriad constellations dancing across the wide-open heavens. Only neither noticed on this occasion. "Are you okay staying by yourself?" he asked.

"I'm staying by myself?"

"Denver and Sarilyn have taken a room in the lodge. Nancy has moved into Hank's shack."

"So I get a bed tonight."

"Want some company?" Eileen glared at him. "It's a two bedroom cabin." Eileen looked away. "For security reasons. No one should be alone."

"I'm looking forward to it. I'm exhausted." They arrived at the women's cabin. Eileen turned toward Richard. "What are we going to do?"

"Find a way out."

"There has to be a way out. Seth and Oscar opened the gate to let us in. There has to be a way for us to open it."

"Unless they disabled it once you arrived. Apparently you completed the team they were assembling. That would take care of one worry." After Eileen gave him a baffled look, he continued. "The trespasser got on the ranch when they opened the gate for you. So if the gate can no longer be opened that means no more trespassers." Seeing the gloom in her face, Richard added, "But we'll keep searching for a way off the ranch."

"Nancy hates me. And the others don't trust me. Including you."

"I trust you. It's Adam I don't trust."

"You think I do? He has information we need. He knows more about this ranch than any of us."

"So you are pumping him?"

"Of course."

"What have you found out?"

Eileen shrugged. "He seems interested in my injured hip." Richard reacted with surprise. "Don't ask me why. Don't ask me anything, I'm so tired I can't think."

"Okay. You've got the walkie-talkie. You'll call if you need anything."

"You're still at the men's cabin?"

"Yes. No one for me to move in with."

Eileen turned and walked to the porch. "No song tonight?"

"I told you Sarilyn moved into the lodge."

"I mean you." Eileen unlocked the front door. "Good night, Richard."

"Good night, Eileen, good night, Eileen, I'll see you in my dreams."

Eileen walked inside and closed and locked the door behind her. She limped into the front bedroom which Sarilyn had vacated. To discover Adam bare-chested beneath the covers, his clothes neatly folded on a chair, smiling idiotically up at her. "Oh God." Eileen collapsed into the chair his clothes were on.

Adam frowned. "I thought we were doing well."

"We're not doing this well."

"Oh. I'm sorry. I'm not very experienced at this."

"At what?"

"Courtship. Dating."

"We haven't dated yet, and you are in my bed naked."

"I've spent my entire life in books, in labs. I've never been intimate with a woman."

"I'm nearly a decade older than you."

"I prefer an older experienced woman. The outdoorsy athletic type. Total opposite of me. In a word, you. Does that bother you?"

Eileen burst out laughing. Seeing Adam staring at her with concern, she tried to explain. "There is a multitude of things bothering me at the moment, but you being attracted to me isn't one of them."

"I should go." Adam turned back the sheet.

"Wait!"

A barely-covered Adam froze. "I shouldn't go?"

"You are naked. So I should go. Then you should go." Eileen struggled to her feet and limped across the room.

"Your limp is worse."

"By the end of the day it gets worse."

"I've got something that might help that."

Intrigued, Eileen stared at him without contempt this time. "Would you like to have a proper date?"

"I would."

"Take me to some interesting places on the ranch tomorrow. I'll bring my camera. Let's meet somewhere away from here."

Adam smiled happily. "Good idea. I upset the others."

"I do, too. How about the cemetery?"

"We have a cemetery?"

"Denver's garden at Sky Lake."

"Nine?"

"Nine." Adam hopped up and walked naked to the chair. When Eileen laughed, he froze in confusion.

"I'm not laughing at you, Adam. Well, actually, I am. But in a good way. Please don't be offended." By the time she got this all out she was guffawing.

A befuddled Adam grabbed his clothes and hurried out.

Hearing the front door open and close, Eileen stopped laughing. She collapsed on the bed and considered her options. Richard and Adam. Both men were interested in her. Which did she prefer? No contest. Adam. He was the most amazing man she had ever met. And she felt so at ease with him. Even when she was wearing only a towel, and even when he was naked. Normally, a man she didn't know that well parading before her would put her off. With Adam she had been relaxed enough to laugh.

Eileen smiled and closed her eyes, to settling into a real bed. She was looking forward to both a good night's sleep on a comfortable mattress and her date with Adam.

Chapter 8 - The Date

The next morning at the appointed time Eileen rode Hell Horse to the garden at Sky Lake. She found Adam standing beside Seth's grave.

"He was sick the first time I met him," Adam informed her. "He got steadily sicker."

Eileen dismounted and joined him at the graveside. "What was wrong with him?"

"Traveler sickness."

"That's what the trespasser said *he* had. What is it?"

"An extreme case of motion sickness, I presume. I haven't experienced it myself." Adam smiled. "On to cheerier things. Your horse will be okay if you leave it here, won't it? There's water and shade."

"We're walking?"

"No. Going by wormhole." Adam laughed when Eileen retreated a step. "It's perfectly safe." When he extended his hand, she shied away. "It's really an experience you shouldn't miss." Adam's hand remained extended until Eileen finally stepped up and grasped it. "Now don't let go. You could get lost." Adam winced when Eileen crushed his hand. "That's it." He led her out of the garden toward the lake. They disappeared in midstride.

Adam led Eileen by the hand through bright white light. She looked all around, but could see nothing but white. She looked down to see she was walking on white. What she stepped on felt firm, but she could see only whiteness. She closed her eyes to concentrate on her other senses. There was no sound whatsoever. She sniffed. Nothing to sniff at. There was no wind, no sense of going either up or down. The air felt the same temperature as it had at the garden. She opened her eyes to check on Adam. He stared straight ahead. So she followed his example and concentrated on the middle of his back.

Adam and Eileen appeared by the pool below Wells Falls. He tried to disengage his hand, but she had an iron grip on it. "It's okay," he said in a soothing voice. "We're out."

Eileen cast terrified looks in all directions. "Where were we?"

Adam took Eileen into his arms. "It's disturbing, at first."

Eileen's trembling legs buckled. "I'm never doing that again."

Adam lowered her to the ground then sat beside her. "Once you're used to it there's no other way to travel. Imagine if you could step into a wormhole in New York and step out of it a minute later in Tokyo. But don't ever try it without me. I know the coordinates. If you ever stumbled into one you would never emerge. You'd wander around lost until you died of thirst."

"That could happen?"

"Theoretically. But the access points are exact. Someone blundering into one is improbable to the nth degree."

Eileen clung to Adam as her tremors subsided and her breathing slowed.

Seeming to enjoy this, he sat still until she eventually raised her head from his chest and looked around to ascertain where she was. "You wanted to use your camera,"

Adam said. "This is a photogenic locale." He stood and pulled Eileen to her feet. He held onto her until she was steady.

She smiled her appreciation. "I'm sorry. That really rocked me."

Adam smiled in return. "You're made of sterner stuff than I. The first time I did it I passed out."

Eileen gave a tension-relieving laugh. "You passed out?"

"Yes. And swore never again, like you. But I'm a scientist. My curiosity got the better of me."

Eileen took her camera from the case slung around her neck. "May I?" She focused on Adam.

He frowned. "There are much prettier sights."

"I don't know. You looked pretty last night. In the buff." Eileen snapped his picture. Then she walked around snapping the waterfall, the pool, the surrounding mountains. Eventually, Eileen turned back toward him. "Why did they kidnap you?"

Having quietly watched her snap so many pictures, he was no longer frowning. "They said they were saving the world."

"From you?"

"Apparently."

"What have you done?"

"I helped some friends cheat on a science project in seventh grade. Other than that, I don't know."

"Did they mistake you for someone else?"

"They seemed sure of what they were doing."

"It doesn't make sense."

"A lot of things on this ranch don't make sense."

"Like their technology. I never knew something like the barrier was possible."

"It's not." When Eileen stared at him, mystified, he smiled. "Did you get enough shots here?"

Eileen scowled. "Are we going back into the wormhole? Already?"

"Would you like to photograph more?"

Eileen gazed at the pool as she put her camera away. "Maybe go for a swim?"

Adam frowned at the pool. "This isn't a good place to swim."

"Why not? The water is warm."

"I know a much better place. But first I'd like to show you my home."

Intrigued, Eileen's scowl slowly faded as Adam extended his hand. With great trepidation she took it. They disappeared.

Eileen clung to Adam as they stepped out of the white into the middle of a small cavern. It was well-lit, filled with tables with scientific apparatus and a computer, and also a narrow bed, refrigerator, microwave, and coffee maker. One picture hung on the wall - the pencil sketch of Eileen standing in the women's cabin wrapped in a towel while Adam stared in adoration up at her from the couch. "I saw Nancy doing this," Eileen said.

"I just had to have it," Adam said. "I swiped it after she moved out. It's amazing how well she paints. Since she came here."

Eileen, with Adam's support, walked over to look at it. "What's going on?"

"Stupidity."

"Nancy's?"

"No. Theirs."

"Seth and Oscar?"

"And the ones who devised this scheme. Monumental stupidity."

"But they seemed to have succeeded in what they set out to do."

Adam laughed with derision. "But there were unintended consequences. There are always unintended consequences. They may have caused the very problem they set out to solve. And now they are trying to solve the consequences. And causing other consequences. Like you."

Eileen drew away from Adam to stare into his face. Still wobbly, she caught herself on the edge of a table. "I'm an unintended consequence of Seth's schemes?"

"Maybe. Or maybe you were intended. I haven't decided yet. Either way, you are here, now, and I like you. So if you were intended perhaps I can turn you to unintended."

"I'm confused."

"What do you think?" Adam swept his arm wide presenting his cavern.

Eileen looked all around. "Stark."

"Functional. I don't require niceties." Adam strode about, and Eileen's gaze followed him. "I'm totally secure here. There is no passage large enough for a person to travel through connecting this cavern to the surface. The only way in and out is through the wormhole."

"Seth let you set all this up here?"

72

"Seth and Oscar have been so ill for so long they lost track of what I was doing. I've practically had a free hand here."

"How do you get power down here?"

"I thought you'd never ask. People always take energy for granted. Just plug it in, flip a switch, charge a battery. But where does it come from? It takes a tremendous amount of energy just to power the barrier. Have you seen any power lines?"

"Perhaps they are buried."

"Out here in the middle of nowhere? On a five-thousand acre ranch? I don't think so. Then how? Have you seen any solar arrays? Wind turbines? Geothermal wells? How did Seth set up an energy supply?"

"Nuclear?"

"Nuclear reactors are huge. Have you seen any? I suppose one could be hidden in the mountains. But it takes a long time to build a nuclear reactor. Seth didn't have that much time."

"Then where is the energy coming from?"

"Have you seen Avatar?"

"What?"

"My favorite movie. Just imagine if that were possible, and there was such a planet." Adam looked Eileen over. "Are you okay?"

"Yes. A little shaky. But not bad. It wasn't so bad this time."

Adam smiled at her. "My, you're strong." He led her away from the table to sit at his desk.

She studied the computer before her. "Do you have Internet access?"

"I wish. There is no access to anything beyond the boundary."

"Hank was picking up a radio station."

Adam was amazed. "Really? How in the world?"

"Some device he'd put together."

"He's an appliance repairman."

"He must be a very good one."

"It's the unobtanium."

"The what?"

"Let me know if he locates the gate. Between the two of us maybe we can get it open."

"So you can go out and destroy the world?"

Adam turned dark as he drew back from her. "Are you taking this prison guard assignment serious?"

"My assignment was for animal husbandry and wildlife biology."

"I'm not spending the rest of my life here. I mean to get off this ranch."

"Me, too."

"Over my dead body?"

"That would be suicide. You said. Have you found out what kind of poison we all drank?"

"I don't care about the poison. I'm not going to kill you. Will you kill me?" Eileen stared blankly at him. He smiled. "You don't have to answer that. Let's go swimming." Adam backed away from the desk.

Eileen stood. "May I take some pictures first?"

"Certainly. Snap away." Adam watched with a contemplative smile, while Eileen photographed more of the cavern.

A few minutes later Adam led Eileen out of the white onto a low hill overlooking a bend in a wide slow-flowing river. The grass was thick and high, and wildflowers abounded in a lush meadow. Tall mountains shimmered in the distance. Another locale in paradise.

Eileen seemed to have taken the trip through the wormhole in stride this time. Adam examined her for ill-effects while she looked around gaining her bearings. "Are you okay?" he asked.

"A little light-headed."

"That's all? I'm impressed. But then you're already a seasoned traveler."

"I haven't traveled that much. I've spent most of my life in Arizona." Eileen took her camera from its case and began taking pictures. "Another beautiful place."

"The bend in the river forms a pool about six feet at its deepest. We are far enough from the mountains for the water to be sun-warmed to a pleasant degree."

"Sounds wonderful." Eileen cut her camera off and put it away then removed the case from around her neck. She sat down in the grass to take off her shoes.

"Are we going barefoot in the grass?" Adam asked.

"More than my feet is getting bare." Eileen stood to unsnap and unzip her jeans. She held onto Adam for support as she stepped out of them. Releasing him to fold her pants, she smiled. "Aren't you joining me?"

"Of course." Adam sat to remove his shoes and watch Eileen take off her blouse. As she walked to the edge of the pool in her underwear, Adam hastily stood to take off his pants. Without anyone to support him, a foot got tangled and he pitched forward to the ground. While Eileen laughed at him sprawled in the grass, Adam sat up and pulled his pants the rest of the way off.

Eileen waded out into the river. "It's cold!" she screamed.

"It's warmer in the middle." Adam stood to yank off his shirt.

Eileen glanced back to see he was joining her. She swam out toward the middle. Treading water, she looked back to him. "You lied! It's still freezing!"

Adam waded in. "It's all in your head."

She splashed him. "You think I'm imagining the cold?" She lunged up above the water as she lifted her bra. "See how big my nipples are? Is that in my head?"

Adam blanched as he grew deathly still. "It's in *my* head now. Forever."

Eileen's bare breasts sank back beneath the water as she pulled her bra back into place. "On the other hand, some things shrink and try to hide from the cold." When she reached inside the front of Adam's undershorts, he sank. "Adam!" She yanked her hand out to grab him by both arms. Kicking furiously, she drug him into shallower water.

Adam stumbled back away from her spitting water. "If you drown me then you'll all die."

"I wasn't trying to drown you. I was just playing with you. I didn't know you were going to stop treading water."

"No woman has ever played with me. Like that."

Eileen smiled as she swam back out to the middle. "Maybe you just need to get used to it."

Adam remained in the shallow water. "Are you talking about the water?"

"Of course. My nipples ache. They're throbbing." Eileen rolled over onto her back. "And your balls were trying to climb up into your rectum to get warm."

Adam hugged himself, shivering, as he watched her do backstrokes.

Later that afternoon Eileen and Adam lay on their backs in the grass beside the river drying in the sun. Eileen basked with eyes closed, while Adam couldn't take his eyes off her. "Tell me about your childhood," he finally broke the silence.

"Tell me about yours."

"Okay. I studied like hell. Now you. What were your parents like?"

"I never knew them. They died in a car wreck while I was a baby."

"Who raised you?"

"People I thought were my parents. When I turned eighteen they said I deserved to know the truth."

"Were you shocked?"

"Surprisingly, no."

Adam smiled grimly. "You believe that old fairy tale?"

"About being of royal lineage and raised by peasants?" Eileen shrugged. "I just didn't seem to fit."

"Common adolescent story."

"More than that. Like my love of animals. We lived in the city, and I wasn't even allowed a pet."

"Have any of your beloved animals ever come to your rescue before? Like your horse did?"

"No. Hell Horse and I bonded quickly." Eileen rolled over onto her stomach. "One side dry."

Adam rolled over, too. "How do you feel about Richard?"

"He's okay."

77

"He was a soldier. Ready to die for his country. Do you think he still feels that way?"

"Yes."

Adam sighed. "I concur. Did you notice his lip?"

"War wound?"

"More likely a poorly-repaired cleft. Military surgeons aren't the best."

Eileen frowned. "Another defect."

"Did you see Nancy's portrait of Hank?"

"Yes. His urethra isn't in the right place."

"The damage to Nancy's right hand wasn't caused by injury or disease. It was a birth defect. Did you notice Denver's flat face? Classic Down Syndrome. Did you see the deformity on Sarilyn's otherwise beautiful back? That day she and Denver were making love in the garden? Spina Bifida Occulta."

"What about you?"

Adam smiled brightly at Eileen. "Do you see any defects?"

"Congratulations."

"But then I haven't travelled as much as you six have."

"What does traveling have to do with birth defects?"

"You wouldn't believe me if I told you. So I won't. Yet."

Realizing she wasn't going to ferret any more information out of him, Eileen closed her eyes. But she could feel Adam's eyes were still open. And on her. Which was what she wanted. For ulterior and manifest motives. She was getting some serious hooks in him. But these hooks seemed to be double-barbed. They hooked her as securely to him. It felt good, this intimacy and

78

playfulness, it felt right. It was getting way too complicated.

Late that afternoon Adam and Eileen, fully dressed and dry, stepped out of the white light into Denver's garden. Hell Horse was grazing nearby in the shade. Adam peered into her face. "Didn't even bat an eye that time."

"Thank you for a fascinating day."

"Is it over?" Adam looked all around. The sun was low. "I lose track of time so easily. Are you hungry? We could go back to the cave to eat."

"No, I'll eat at the lodge."

"Don't blame you. Nancy is such a good cook."

Eileen started toward her horse.

"Wait."

Eileen stopped and looked back.

"Let's try an experiment. Call your horse. Instead of walking to him. See if he'll come."

Eileen looked to her horse and whistled. The horse trotted toward her. She looked back to Adam.

"See those geese out on the lake? Call to them."

Eileen looked queerly at him.

"Try it."

Eileen whistled once again. The geese took wing and flew toward her. She watched in amazement as they landed at her feet.

"I saw a fox out here earlier. Try calling to him."

Eileen looked all around. "I don't see a fox."

"See if he'll come even if you can't see him. Try it."

Eileen whistled once again. Nothing happened. "I guess I'm not as powerful as you think I am."

"Wait." They stood silent for a moment.

Until a black bear topped a nearby hill. Surprisingly, the horse and geese remained calm as it strolled down the hill into the garden. But Eileen didn't. She scrambled up on her horse. "Some fox! Climb on behind me!"

"The bear won't hurt you." Eileen calmed as the bear approached her horse. Amazingly, the horse remained calmer than Eileen. "I don't think he'll hurt me, either. Unless you want him to."

"You think I could do that?"

"Could? Yes. Would? I don't know."

"Why would I want to hurt you?"

"Because you were designed to. To complete me and to destroy me. Goodbye, Eileen." Adam disappeared. Leaving Eileen looking around at her strange menagerie.

Chapter 9 - The Other Movie

Later that afternoon Eileen was ambushed by Denver and Sarilyn when she walked out of the barn after stabling Hell Horse. Denver grabbed her and slammed her against the side of the barn. He waved a gun in her face. "Richard told me what happened to the trespasser. Your horse comes out here and I shoot it." Inside the barn all the horses went wild.

Sarilyn thrust her enraged face up to Eileen's bewildered face. "What were you and Adam doing all day?!"

Eileen struggled to compose herself, but Denver didn't give her a chance to. He slammed her against the side of the barn again. "Henry and Nancy were murdered. Beat to death."

"By you and Adam!" Sarilyn accused.

Eileen finally caught enough breath to respond. "That's crazy."

"No one else is here!" Sarilyn said. "It had to been him! And you were with him all day!"

Denver raised his gun to pistol whip Eileen. "Tell us!"

A large hawk swooped down and raked Denver's face with its talons. Denver screamed as he dropped his gun and grabbed his slashed face with both hands.

Eileen snatched up the gun and trained it on the pair. The hawk landed on her shoulder.

Sarilyn hugged Denver as he sobbed in pain. "What kind of witch are you?"

81

"The kind you don't want to mess with," Richard said upon joining them. He holstered his gun. "Are you going to shoot us now?"

"I was attacked!"

"Why don't you go calm your horse down." Hell Horse was raising the loudest ruckus in the barn.

Eileen turned to Denver and Sarilyn. "I'm keeping this gun. Don't jump me like that again." She walked into the barn to settle all the horses. The hawk flew up to perch on the barn roof, from where it could keep watch on the three below.

A moment later Richard entered the barn. "There's not a rattlesnake in here that's going to jump up and bite me, is there?"

"There could be."

"Denver's face is a mess."

"He was about to make a mess out of *my* face. Besides, I didn't do that."

"No, the hawk did it for you."

"I don't know why that happens." Eileen turned her attention back to her horse. "Henry and Nancy are dead?"

"Yes. We found them in Henry's shack. Which was ransacked. The trespasser's gun is gone. So is the device Henry was working on to locate the gate. Things Adam would be interested in."

"Are you sure there isn't another trespasser? Because Adam was with me all day."

"I know you were with him at least part of the day. I saw you swimming in Bright Creek."

"Enjoy the show?"

"Wasn't much of a show. All you did was swim."

"Adam claims we've all got poisons in us that keeps us from killing each other. Is he lying?"

"We've got some foreign substance in our blood. Sarilyn isolated it. But she has no idea what it is."

"So he could be telling the truth. What about Oscar? Any trace of him?"

"No. But he never harmed any of us before. Why should he now?"

Eileen continued soothing her horse. "I'm sorry about Hank and Nancy. But if Adam has some poison in his blood that keeps him from killing us how could he murder them?"

"It's in *our* blood. We don't have a sample of Adam's blood to check. Or yours, since you just got here."

"I'm not letting Sarilyn near me with a needle. Not after what just happened."

"So maybe you could have killed them."

Eileen spun to confront him angrily. "Do I look like someone who could beat two people to death?"

"You're a dangerous person to be around, that's for sure." Richard sighed heavily. "But we didn't find any hoof or paw prints around the shack."

"That's reassuring."

"It could be another trespasser, like you said. Or even Oscar. We can't find him anywhere. But I did find something interesting. Seth's movie. He had it backed up on a laptop he'd hidden."

"Can't hide anything from you for long. Not with your eyes."

"I know. We've all turned weird since coming here." Richard walked away toward the door. "It's at the Men's cabin." Eileen fell in step behind him.

As they walked out of the barn there was no sign of Denver or Sarilyn. "I'm sorry about what happened to Denver."

"He's a hothead. I told him you couldn't have done it."

"After what just happened I'm sure he's convinced I did."

Richard looked up at the hawk still perched atop the barn and raised both arms high. "I'm not touching her. Okay? I'm not hurting her." When Eileen laughed as they continued to the men's cabin, he said, "That's good. Keep laughing."

Richard and Eileen sat at the kitchen table before a laptop. On the screen Seth, as sick as ever, sat behind his desk in his office at the lodge. Seated behind him was Oscar. They both faced the screen. Richard unpaused the frozen image. "Hello Richard, Henry, Denver, Nancy, Sarilyn, Eileen. If you are watching this then I am dead. In that event there are things you need to know. Adam is a brilliant unscrupulous young man who will destroy ninety-five per cent of the world's population. The damage he caused has so warped reality that wormholes to the recent past open briefly and unpredictably. It is through one of these wormholes that I and Oscar traveled to this time when Adam was a young man. We came to prevent Adam from wreaking havoc on our world. We could not execute him since we have outlawed capital punishment. Besides, how could we justify it? He has not done anything at this point in his life to merit death. So a decision was made to isolate him. I and Oscar set up this prison, brought Adam here, then enticed you six here to guard him after we died. We've learned the human body

84

was not designed to travel through time. Learned the hard way. But perhaps our deaths have saved our world from near destruction. If so, then we died honorably. Hopefully, you six will serve as honorably.

"We prepared this ranch to make you as comfortable as possible. And you were chosen for your compatibility. You should live long fruitful lives here. The unobtanium that powers the barrier will exhaust itself in a hundred years, long after Adam's death. So your children and grandchildren will be free to go. But Adam cannot kill you. Upon your arrival you each drank fluids which contained nano-transmitters that will activate a powerful poison in Adam upon your death by his hands. The nanotechnology is intelligent enough to determine the cause of death, so only murder by Adam will activate it. This was designed to protect you against Adam, while protecting Adam against your death by accident or disease.

"I know this must seem a harsh sentence on you, but you are doing vital work. You are saving our world from Armageddon. So guard Adam carefully. He must not be allowed to escape the ranch. For if he does it will mean the near total destruction of the world. Our world. Your world. The end of nearly everything." The screen went blank.

Richard and Eileen sat staring at the blankness. "We're trapped here," Richard said. "With Adam."

"Until he figures out a way to escape."

Richard leaned back from the screen to look at Eileen. "Do you think he can?"

"He's already manipulated the barrier to create his own wormholes. That's how he appears and disappears."

"He can't make a wormhole through the barrier?"

"Not yet." Eileen stood to pace. "Time travelers. It's too much." She stopped to peer at Richard. "So Adam couldn't have murdered Hank and Nancy. It would kill him."

"I agree. But Seth didn't say anything about us not being able to kill Adam. He made that part up to protect himself."

"They won't execute Adam. But they wouldn't mind if we did it for them. Phony liberals."

Richard changed the subject. "Do you know anything about unobtanium?"

"Adam mentioned it. Did you see Avatar?"

"Of course. In the movie unobtanium was an incredible power source found only on the planet Pandora."

"Adam said it was his favorite movie. He also keeps saying something else interesting. That people are as stupid as ever."

"I'm sure he believes no one is half as intelligent as he is. Not even people from the future." Richard stood. "Have you eaten?"

"I'm not hungry."

"We've got to keep our strength up. If we're to save the world."

"So you are accepting the mission?"

"I'm a soldier. I was prepared to lay down my life for my country on the battlefield. This isn't such a bad battlefield. I've seen much worse." Richard smiled. "Besides, we get to have children." Faced with Eileen's grimace, he continued. "Or not. Anyway, I think you

86

should stay here. Somebody brutally murdered Nancy and Henry. We're safer together."

"Being together didn't help Hank and Nancy."

"Hank wasn't a highly trained security specialist."

"Who can see and hear for miles."

"And Nancy wasn't a beast master who can rally animals to her defense. We'll be tougher to kill." Richard went to the refrigerator to see what he could find for dinner. "I will miss Nancy's cooking."

"If *you* are going to cook," Eileen replied, "then you won't miss Nancy as much as I will."

Chapter 10 - With Richard

Late that night Eileen was blasted out of her sleep when the world erupted outside her window. She lurched up out of bed to the window to see that the remnants of the lodge were ablaze. Pieces of flaming logs were strewn across the night. A small fire lit up the front of the men's cabin from a piece of log that had landed ten feet away.

The bedroom door burst open and Richard ran in to join her at the window. They both gazed bleakly at the inferno. "Oh, God," Eileen moaned. "Denver and Sarilyn."

"They're okay. Denver told me they were hiding out. They didn't feel safe at the lodge."

"Thank God. Where are they?"

Richard gave her a dark look. "He didn't tell me and I didn't ask." He backed away from the window. "Let's go."

Eileen continued to stare at the blaze. "Where?"

"Somewhere safer than this." Richard gathered up Eileen's clothes and tossed them to her.

Only then did she realize they were both in only their underpants. Eileen doubled her arms across her chest as she scowled at Richard. "If you want me to go anywhere with you don't burst in on me like this."

Richard glared at her. "You're kidding! The lodge just blew up and you're worried about me seeing your tits?"

Eileen turned her back on him. "Get out so I can get dressed."

"It sure didn't bother you with Adam seeing them."

"I've got Denver's gun. Next time you charge into my bedroom in the middle of the night I just might be scared enough to blow your head off."

Richard drew a deep breath then released it. "I'm going out to see if there is any burning wood on the cabin roof." Echoes from the slammed bedroom door followed Richard out.

After dressing, Eileen emerged from the men's cabin to find Richard prowling around. "Everything is wet and green and there isn't any wind. The fires should go out without spreading."

Eileen looked to the burning lodge. The flames were already less intense. "Do you think someone blew it up?"

"With all that's going on? Of course."

"It couldn't have been Adam. That would be attempting suicide."

"Then someone else from the future is here. Another trespasser."

"He was from the future?"

"Seth said there were wormholes through time. And I've never seen a gun like the last trespasser had. And he was dying from the effects of time travel. Just like Seth and Oscar."

"So someone else has come back to kill us?"

"And maybe to break Adam out of prison."

"So there are time travelers who want to help Adam?"

"Could be. Or maybe some people from the future aren't so squeamish about executions and have come to kill him. And us. To clean up an operation they see as failing."

89

"I was sound asleep when the lodge blew up. Do you trust me now?"

"No. But I need you." Richard walked back toward the cabin. "Let's get back inside. We're too exposed in the firelight."

Eileen cast a wary glance all around the surrounding dark, then followed Richard into the cabin.

Daylight graced Eileen's eyes next time they opened. She was swaddled in a sleeping bag on a bare wooden floor. There was an empty sleeping bag beside her. Eileen crawled out of her bag and limped to the open door. She saw the Jeep parked next to the cabin by the hot springs where she had encountered the trespasser. A short ways off she saw Richard peering off into the distance. He glanced back at her. "Someone's coming."

"It's not Adam," Eileen said as she joined him. "He would just appear here through one of his wormholes. Another trespasser?"

Richard handed her the binoculars. After focusing them she could see what Richard had seen with his bare eyes. "Oscar."

"He looks perfectly healthy now," Richard answered.

"Adam cured him?"

"And turned him to be his hit man. He's the one who beat Henry and Nancy to death and tried to kill Denver and Sarilyn by blowing up the lodge."

"So Oscar could kill us," Eileen said. "Without Adam having to do it himself." When Richard raised his rifle, without bothering with the sight, Eileen put her hand on the barrel and forced it down. "Wait. I've got a better way." She whistled.

Richard grabbed her. "What are you doing?!"

Hearing her whistle, Oscar stopped in his tracks and looked toward them. Then ran toward them. Richard raised his gun again.

"Wait. Can you hear it? I can't, but you should be able to."

Richard froze. He obviously heard something.

A herd of bison charged up over a near ridge and stampeded down toward Oscar. Oscar turned to face them, but it was too late. He disappeared beneath their rampaging hoofs. After trampling Oscar, the bison continued charging up the ridge toward Richard and Eileen.

Richard raised his gun to fire, but Eileen pushed the barrel down and stepped in front of him. Richard stepped up directly behind her, the herd of bison parted and ran around Eileen.

After the last maddened bison passed, Richard stepped back from Eileen. While he stood shaking, Eileen limped down the ridge toward Oscar's broken body. Richard took a deep calming breath before following. She had nearly reached the body by the time he was steady enough to go after her.

Eileen stooped beside Oscar. Electronics were exposed beneath his ripped open skin.

Richard joined Eileen. "A robot. No wonder he didn't want Sarilyn to examine him."

"So even a robot couldn't travel through time without damage?" Eileen asked.

Richard poked around the corpse. "Or some kind of an android. There's a lot of human tissue here with all the electronics." He turned back to Eileen. "Whatever he was, Adam repaired him. And reprogrammed him."

91

Eileen picked up the trespasser's gun from the ground beside Oscar's body. As she looked it over it once again came to life in her grasp. "Tough material. Hardly a scratch."

"So why didn't he use it against them?"

"It's not programmed for him." Eileen aimed the gun at a nearby tree and fired. An energy beam struck the tree. The tree exploded.

"Impressive," Richard noted.

Eileen lowered the gun. "What if the trespasser Hell Horse trampled didn't come here to kill us, or Adam? What if he knew he would be too weak to do much of anything?"

"A suicide mission?"

"Like Seth's. What if he came here to deliver this gun to me? This gun and a message?"

"The Dick line? To you? Why?"

"Maybe it was a code. To activate me. To kill Adam." Eileen held the still-glowing gun up to admire it.

92

Chapter 11 - With Adam

Richard and Eileen drove the Jeep to Wells Falls. Eileen climbed out with Denver's gun in hand and the trespasser's gun in the waistband of her pants, and Richard climbed out with a gun holstered on his hip and a rifle in hand.. "Why do you think he's here?" Richard asked.

"I think the unobtanium is here." Eileen pointed at the pool. "Down there. Look closely, Richard."

Richard peered into the depths. "I see something glowing at the bottom. How did you know?"

"The water is warm when it should be icy. All the hot springs on the ranch are marked on the map. There is no hot spring marked on the map for here. Adam said this isn't a good place to swim despite it seeming a perfect place. The water here is much warmer than the water where he took me to swim. Perhaps there is radiation in the water? Because the unobtanium needs to be cooled? That could be a good reason for not swimming here."

Adam stepped out from behind the waterfall. "Are you really that smart, Eileen? Or did the trespasser awaken hidden knowledge in you?

Richard raised his rifle, but Eileen stepped in front of him to face Adam. "What am I?"

"Everything in a woman I ever dreamed of. Your hair, your smile, your build, your bearing, your voice, your eyes. Your bone structure, for Christ's sake. Your mouth, your nose. An ideal mate. For me."

Richard lowered his gun and looked from Eileen to Adam. "What are you talking about?"

"Eileen was designed for me, Richard. In the future. And sent back as a baby. Apparently babies can make it back through time without dying."

"Except it causes damage. Like my hip."

"Yes. The people who adopted you had no idea what caused the injury. So they made up the story about falling off a horse. A child needs some kind of a story."

"What do you mean she was designed? For you?"

"Eileen was conceived in a petri dish. Everything in a woman that appeals to me was designed into her."

"So that you would fall for me. Let me get close to you."

"Close enough to kill me. They designed the perfect assassin. One tailored to attract its target. This was their last resort. Once they saw their original plan falling apart. The idiots. Of course it fell apart."

Richard appeared stunned. "Eileen is an assassin designed in a lab of the future and sent back through time as a baby to grow up and kill you."

"Eileen was only one of six names Seth had to contact and bring here. He had no idea what she was. He believed they were only trying to imprison me. To isolate me from the world."

"What did you do?" Richard asked.

"I haven't done it yet so how could I know?"

"You called them idiots. Why?" Eileen asked. "Why do you believe them to be so stupid?"

"Technological advances make people stupid. How are your math skills? Who cares, you've got a calculator. How good is your spelling? Doesn't matter, you've got a spell checker. How about your sense of direction? Why worry, you've got satellite navigation. How many facts

94

have you committed to memory? Why bother, you've got Google. And I'm sure it gets much worse in the future. It's like there is a law of physics at work, the conservation of intelligence. There is only so much in the world, so as devices get smarter people get dumber."

"So you're saying they didn't plan very well."

"They sent unobtanium back as the power source for the ranch. Without realizing what it would do to us."

"Is that the reason we are like we are?"

"Yes. The people in the future, like Seth, have grown up with it. They're immune to its effects. But I have never been exposed to it before, you only briefly as a baby."

"Is that what enhances our natural abilities?"

"And what is my natural ability?"

"Your intelligence. So by exposing you to unobtanium..."

"...they raised my intelligence to a level where I could devise a way to destroy the world. Which I never would have been intelligent enough to do if I hadn't been exposed to the unobtanium."

"So they brought about the destruction of the world with their plan to prevent it. The solution to the problem is the problem."

"But we can still fix things." Richard raised his rifle.

Adam merely smiled. "Where are Denver and Sarilyn? Have you heard from them today?"

"What have you done with them?" Richard demanded.

"Lured them into my maze of wormholes. Without food or water. Kill me and they will never escape. They'll die a slow agonizing death. There is no way out for them."

"You can't kill us now," Eileen said. "We destroyed your assassin."

"Oscar had instructions only to kill Richard. He wouldn't have harmed you, Eileen."

Richard lowered his rifle. "So we are at an impasse."

"Yes. Now we negotiate."

"Or not." Eileen aimed Denver's gun at Adam. "What if I decide the death of two people I don't especially like is acceptable? To save the world?"

"But what if they're wrong, Eileen?" Adam said. "They've been wrong about so much. What if I'm wrong? What if you're wrong?"

"How?"

"What if you were sent to stop me from destroying the world by means other than killing me? Think about it. Seth could have killed me at any time. But his morality wouldn't allow him to. So maybe you weren't intended to kill me, either. Maybe you were meant to stop me by loving me. Would I destroy a world in which I had a stake in? Sons and daughters, grandchildren? Not only were you designed to attract me, but also to be attracted *by* me." When Eileen lowered the gun, Adam approached her.

"Don't let him have the trespasser's gun," Richard said. Eileen backed away and trained the gun on Adam once again.

He halted. "Why would I want it? It's no use to me."

"You broke the security on it so Oscar could use it to blow up the lodge," Richard said.

"Oscar didn't use the gun. I examined it after he brought it to me. But I couldn't alter it. That gun was engineered to recognize Eileen. It will work only for her."

"Then why did he have it with him?"

"To give back to Eileen. After he had killed you. As a show of faith."

"Then how did Oscar blow up the lodge?"

"With a milligram of unobtanium. Once I located the power source for the ranch. Down there." Adam indicated the pool. "I swam down and scraped off a sliver of it. Studied it."

"And figured out how to weaponize it," Richard said.

"Yes."

"So that's how you do it," Eileen said.

"Do what?"

"Destroy the world. By turning unobtanium into a weapon."

Adam froze. "Do you really think so?"

"You probably even named it. Seth called it unobtanium in his video."

"Could I have?"

"Say you escape from the ranch with the unobtanium, present the world with this incredible new power source, then it gets turned into a weapon and unleashed."

Adam laughed hysterically. "Of course! It would fit! They are so stupid! They would have handed me the means of their own destruction!" Adam quit laughing. He stared longingly at Eileen. "Except I would never abandon you. If their plan was to entrap me with you then it succeeded. Maybe they aren't so stupid." He extended his hand. "Come with me. Your life will be empty without me. As mine will be without you. We were literally made for each other."

Richard looked to Eileen. "Don't listen to him. He's treacherous."

"But he's right. I was made for him." Eileen lowered the gun and walked toward Adam.

"You don't know that! It could all be a pack of lies!"

"But I do know it."

"Philip K. Dick told her," Adam said.

Richard raised his gun at Adam. "I won't let you take her away."

Eileen stepped between Adam and Richard. "You'll have to shoot me to stop me, Richard."

Richard's hand wavered as his face collapsed. "It wasn't supposed to be like this."

"Yes, I know," Adam said. "You thought it was supposed to be you and Eileen, and the others, three happy couples." Adam took Eileen's hand that held the trespasser's gun. "Let's go back to my cavern."

"What about Denver and Sarilyn?" she asked.

"I'll release them. Come with me and they'll be free."

Eileen looked back to Richard. "I'll be okay, Richard. Adam won't hurt me."

"My, he's certainly taking this hard," Adam said.

Eileen stared at Richard with compassion. "I know." Adam pulled Eileen along as he stepped back. They disappeared into a wormhole.

Adam led Eileen out of the whiteness into his cavern. No longer disturbed travelling by wormhole, she looked all around. "Where are they?"

"I have no idea. Somewhere on the ranch."

"Another lie."

"Another?"

"Like the poison that would kill us if we were to kill you."

Adam chuckled. "I had to give you pause." Adam enveloped Eileen in his arms.

She pulled away. "You lie to me too much."

"Self-preservation. You might be meant to kill me." Eileen strolled about the cavern looking at this and that, while Adam looked only at her. "Richard is in love with you."

"We hardly know each other. We just met this week."

"I was crazy about you the minute I saw you."

"But that was designed to happen."

"A fact you seem to be taking well. Unless you don't really believe it."

"Oh, I believe it. I feel the attraction to you in my bones. It must be the effect of the Dick code. Things have been coming to me in small doses, in amounts I can handle."

"To keep you from going into shock or becoming suicidal. Clever."

"For such stupid people."

"But don't you agree? Their plans..."

"What about me? I'm part of their plans. Was it stupid?"

Adam approached her. "Not if it works. And it can work by you staying with me."

"On the ranch?"

"No. We'll get off this damn ranch. Maybe blast through the gate with that gun of yours. Once I locate the gate with Henry's device."

"Does his device work?"

"It will once I finish improving it." Adam released her and went to his worktable. The device was spread out in pieces.

"You said you had something that could help my hip? Or was that a lie, too?"

Adam's face lit up. "No, I do. Take off your pants." When Eileen glared at him, he continued, "I have to get at your hip." Adam rummaged around a cabinet.

Eileen set Denver's gun aside and pulled out the trespasser's gun to set beside it. She took off her jeans and draped them across the back of a chair. When Adam walked up to her with a jar of mud, she asked, "What is that?"

"Mud from the bottom of the pool. I dug it up when I dove down for the unobtanium."

"Why?"

"Because it's had prolonged exposure to intense unobtanium radiation." Eileen looked at it skeptically. "I've studied it. Modified it. Improved it. It has miraculous qualities. I've already used it successfully once. On Oscar. Lay down on my bed. On your good side with your injured hip up." Once Eileen did as instructed, Adam knelt beside the bed and pulled her panties down to expose her upturned hip. He thoroughly enjoyed the task of rubbing the mud into her hip.

Eileen closed her eyes with a sigh of pleasure. "My body comes alive wherever you touch it."

"You were well-designed," he said as he massaged her hip. "To respond to me."

"Do you think this can help the others?" she asked.

"I don't know."

"But why? Why do we all have defects?"

"It could be a variation of traveler sickness. Or maybe you six were born into a world on the verge of

100

collapse. An environment harsh on a pregnant woman and the fetus inside her."

Eileen's eyes popped open and grew wide. "It's working."

Adam stopped to look hopefully into her smiling face. "Already?"

"It *is* working!" Eileen touched the mud herself and held up fingers coated with it before her eyes. "Adam! What have you done?" Eileen pulled up her panties as she sprang to her feet. She pranced nimbly across the cavern and bounced on her toes and jumped. All without the slightest limp. "It feels wonderful!" Smiling brilliantly, Eileen ran up and threw herself on Adam. They toppled back onto the bed with Eileen on top smothering him with kisses. "Thank you! Thank you! Thank you!" She stopped and drew back to stare into his face. "Will it last?"

"I don't know. We'll apply more if needed. There's plenty of the stuff."

Eileen hugged him one final time then scrambled up. "Let's go tell the others."

Adam's happiness faded. "Why?"

Eileen grabbed her pants and leaped into them. "This could be a miracle cure for who knows what."

"Shouldn't we wait and see?"

"We'll wait. We can't just walk off the ranch. It will take time to escape. But don't you see? You'll be famous. And rich. And renowned, and loved and admired, and all that. A Nobel Prize in medicine. Adam! We'll be so happy!" Eileen pulled Adam to his feet. "We've got to tell the others!"

Adam frowned at her. "The last time I saw Richard he was threatening me with a gun."

101

"I won't let him hurt you. Please!"

Adam studied her glowing face another moment. "I can't refuse you, Eileen."

She snatched up the jar of mud and happily jammed the trespasser's gun back into the waistband of her jeans.

Adam smiled faintly as he looked at her beaming face. "And you know that." He stepped forward and pulled her with him into a wormhole.

Chapter 12 - Freedom

Adam and Eileen stepped out of the white before the waterfall.

"They're here!"

Both spun around to find Denver aiming a rifle at them. Adam was stunned, Eileen so surprised she dropped the jar of mud. "How did you find your way out?" Adam asked.

"Do you really think my enhanced skill is gardening?" Denver answered. "I enjoy it, I'm good at it. But my passion is exploring."

"You found a way out with your enhanced sense of direction," Adam said.

"Out from where?" Eileen asked Adam. "You said you didn't know where they were."

"Out from his wormholes," Denver said. "He tricked me and Sarilyn into one then abandoned us."

Sarilyn stepped up alongside Denver with a revolver aimed at them. "He left us there to die."

"I was coming back for you," Adam said.

Eileen stepped away from him. "You lied to me. Again."

"Eileen, I..."

Richard rushed up and grabbed Eileen from behind. He drug her away toward the pool.

"I've got you covered," Denver said to Richard. To Sarilyn he said, "Shoot him if he moves."

Sarilyn stepped up with her gun aimed at Adam. "Gladly."

"Eileen!" Adam exclaimed. "I won't lie to you again!"

Richard hustled Eileen toward the pool.

Denver, with rifle raised, turned in circles looking all around.

"Richard," Eileen asked. "What are you doing?"

"Getting us out of here. Take the trespasser gun out."

"Why?"

"Because it only works for you. Take it out." Eileen fumbled the gun from out of her jeans. The gun came to life, as usual.

"You'll blow us all to hell," Adam warned.

Sarilyn glanced doubtfully at Richard. "You said it wouldn't."

"Ha!" Adam barked. "One milligram blew up the lodge. Imagine what setting off the entire deposit will do."

"It hasn't been weaponized," Richard said. "It's like unrefined uranium. It won't blow up." Richard gripped Eileen's hands in both of his. He forced her finger onto the trigger.

"Then why does the unobtanium need to be cooled?" Adam asked.

"No!" Eileen refused.

"It's our only chance," Richard insisted. He forced the barrel down toward the water.

Eileen struggled against him. "How do you know it won't blow up?"

"I know." Richard shoved Eileen to the edge of the pool. "I can see it, Eileen. Sitting on the bottom. I'll aim the gun. You pull the trigger."

A wolf charged out of the rocks and leaped toward Richard. Denver fired his rifle. The wolf was blasted back into the rocks. Sarilyn watched as Denver walk up and kill the wolf with a second shot.

Adam lunged backwards while Sarilyn was distracted. She spun back around and fired, but he had disappeared into a wormhole. The bullet flew through empty air.

"Now!" Richard yelled, forcing the gun down toward a target only he could see. "Before any more wild animals show up. Do it now." He forced his finger over her finger on the trigger. He tried to squeeze the trigger by squeezing her finger. The gun wouldn't fire.

Until Eileen squeezed the trigger herself. A beam shot down into the pool through the water to the bottom. Then the beam went out.

Richard released Eileen and stepped back looking all around with apprehensive expectation. Eileen, Denver and Sarilyn all lowered their guns to look around, also. "It didn't work," Denver said.

Eileen stared incredulously at Richard. "Can't you feel it?"

Richard looked back to her. "Feel what?"

"How far can you see?"

Richard looked all around then held still as if listening. His face was screwed up with the intensity of his effort. A few seconds later his face relaxed into a smile. "Not beyond the end of my nose."

Denver and Sarilyn scrambled down the rocks to join Richard and Eileen by the pool. "What's going on?" Denver asked.

"It worked," Richard answered. "Her gun knocked out the unobtanium. Sing us a song, Sarilyn."

She stared at him like he was insane. "I'm not singing."

"Denver, make her sing."

"Anything, Sarilyn," Denver urged, smiling. "Just try."

Sarilyn sighed. Took a deep breath. As she began to sing her voice cracked. She stopped singing and looked around in confusion.

Eileen held up the trespasser gun. It no longer glowed or hummed. "The gun's dead, too," she said. "It must have been powered by the unobtanium."

"Great," Denver said. "We were going to blast a hole in the barrier with it."

"Denver," Richard answered him. "The barrier was powered by the unobtanium."

Denver's smile grew larger by the second. "So the barrier is down?"

"Let's go find out," Richard said.

"What about Adam?" Sarilyn asked.

Richard's face darkened. "I've got a bad feeling about him." He jogged away from the pool up the hillside onto the highest rock and raised his binoculars.

"Need binoculars now, old man?" Eileen asked as Richard scanned the countryside. Then she smiled at Sarilyn. "Look, Sarilyn." Eileen danced, moving agilely about the pool. "My limp is gone. Adam cured me."

Denver jogged up to the rock Richard was perched on. "Do you see him?"

"Yes." Richard handed the binoculars to Denver. He climbed down and walked toward Eileen with a solemn expression.

Denver scanned the distance. "Damn. What happened to him?"

"His wormholes must have been powered by the unobtanium. Without power they collapsed."

"With Adam inside," Denver continued.

"Yes." Richard arrived at Eileen's side.

Sarilyn scrambled up the rocks and took the binoculars from Denver. "Adam is dead?"

He guided the binoculars for her. "Scattered across the ranch in a hundred pieces."

"Mission accomplished," Eileen calmly walked away from Richard.

"Damn," Sarilyn exclaimed as she scanned the countryside with the binoculars. "Is all that Adam?"

"You're taking this awfully well," Richard said. "And walking awfully well."

Eileen stooped to retrieve the jar of mud and put the lid back on. "How did you know this would work?"

Richard walked over to her. "Ubik darkly scans Palmer Eldritch."

Eileen stared in wonder at him. "The Dick code was for you, too?" Acknowledging his nod, she continued. "I passed out when I heard it. But you didn't bat an eye when I said it to you."

"I'm a soldier. I'm more circumspect with my reactions."

Eileen glanced at his upper lip. "So that's not a war wound?"

"My adoptive parents were more truthful than yours. They told me it was cleft the first time I asked about it."

"What was that?" Denver asked. He had left Sarilyn with the binoculars to join Richard and Eileen. "Ubik what?"

Eileen and Richard had been so intent on each other they hadn't noticed Denver's approach. Eileen replied, "Ubik darkly..."

"Never mind," Richard cut her off. "It's just foolishness."

Denver looked from him to Eileen.

His attention was diverted by Sarilyn. "Ewww! I see part of his head!"

Denver jogged back over to the rock Sarilyn was perched on. "Haven't you seen enough?"

Eileen turned back to Richard. "Why did you stop me?"

"What if they're like us? Possess secret knowledge? That just hasn't been activated by the code yet."

Eileen stared at Denver and Sarilyn in wonder. "You mean all six of us? How would they know we would all live long enough to come here? You fought in two wars."

"Maybe they sent back dozens of babies and we're the survivors. But it doesn't matter now. Like you said, mission accomplished. So why complicate their lives? They seem happy together. Let their hidden knowledge stay hidden." He glanced to see Denver helping Sarilyn down off the rock. "How about us? Can we be happy together? We know what we are. Would you want to share that knowledge with anyone else?"

"You just killed the man I loved."

"Was programmed to love. Besides, I didn't murder Adam. If he hadn't run back into his wormhole, he'd still be alive."

"I was designed to kill him. Or I was designed to love him. Either way, now that he's dead I no longer feel anything for him. Maybe I wasn't designed to feel anything for anyone else."

"We can explore that bleak possibility. What have you got there?"

Eileen held up the jar of mud. "This could do a lot of good. And make us a lot of money."

"Let's go!" Denver exclaimed as he and Sarilyn walked off toward the Jeep. When Richard and Eileen caught up, he asked, "Did I hear you mention a lot of money?"

Eileen lowered the jar of mud. "But we can't."

"Why can't we?"

"Adam created this. What if this is what destroys the world? You saw what a little bit of the unobtanium did to the lodge. The prediction of Adam destroying the world could still come true."

"Then leave it," Richard said.

"But it cured my hip! Look!" Eileen pirouetted before him. "It could be a miracle cure for a lot of incurable conditions. And I know where to get more. The bottom of the pool is filled with mud irradiated by unobtanium."

"We'll study it," Richard said. "See what happens to you. Without revealing it."

"It would be much easier turning it over to a lab for study. After obtaining patents on it, of course."

"It would be much easier to kill you."

Eileen froze, staring at Richard's dark expression.

"You no longer have any animals protecting you." His glare resolved into a smile.

"I don't think you're kidding," Eileen said, despite his smile.

"Maybe I was designed in a lab, too, like you. Only for a different purpose. Maybe I was designed to protect the world. Whatever it takes. I was a very good soldier."

Eileen withdrew several paces from his side. "I'll keep that in mind."

Arriving at the Jeep, Denver picked up a piece of a finger from the hood. Sarilyn made a face as he flung it away. The four climbed into the Jeep and drove off.

The Jeep grew smaller and smaller as it bounced away into the distance. While mud that had slopped out of the jar where Eileen dropped it began to bubble and eat into the rock. A noxious cloud arose.

THE END